The Fifth Britain

Modern Magick, 4

Charlotte E. English

1

I USED TO READ a lot of Enid Blyton books as a child. They were about close-knit families and groups of friends, who, despite occasional bouts of quarrelsome behaviour, were very much All In It Together. Those children had siblings and loving parents and stable homes — all of it — but! They were still allowed to spend all day rambling about having adventures. Of course I adored them.

Whenever I was particularly lonely, I used to make up my own adventures. They featured me as the heroine, of course, surrounded by a fine crew of loyal chums, and we spent our time solving crimes and mysteries, uncovering long-lost spells, saving beleaguered beasts, travelling to magickal realms, and generally getting into all kinds of productive trouble. (I like that term: "productive trouble".

I must remember it for the next time Jay gets all raised-eyebrows at me).

Anyway, a good adventure story always begins with a snappy title. *Five Go To Mystery Moor. Five Get Into a Fix. Look Out Secret Seven.* Mine had titles like *Six Go To Honeycup Dell* and *Six Cast a Spell*, which to be fair were not as jazzy as they could've been but what do you want from me, I was ten.

If ten-year-old Ves could have peeped ahead twenty years at what thirty-year-old Ves would be doing, she might have fainted with delight.

'How about *Three Go Rogue*?' I mused aloud. I was speaking for the benefit of Jay and Zareen, my only companions that morning. It wasn't even nine o' clock yet, though the sun was already high, it being late in May. We were huddled around a table in a coffee shop not far from Home (forgive me if I don't say precisely where. The best adventures have their secrets, too).

Jay just looked at me. He had a pole-axed air which I could not quite like, partly because the lost look in his dark eyes unpleasantly echoed the shameful clenched feeling in my own belly. This is not how an adventurer responds to a surprise! A little constructive adversity is bread and butter to a former member of the Splendid Six. This was exciting. This was *thrilling*.

Terrifying, said a small part of my mind, which I instantly and ruthlessly squashed.

'What?' said Jay.

'Three Go Rogue,' I repeated. 'Though I am having trouble coming up with a suitably alliterative nickname for the three of us. It would be much more convenient if we numbered four.'

'The Thrifty Three,' offered Zareen, without looking up. She, alone of the three of us, appeared untouched by the suddenness with which we had been evicted from Home. She was as unruffled as ever, and had already dispatched two cups of coffee and a large breakfast. I had forced my way through a couple of pastries because the old, sunnily untroubled Ves would have done so with relish. I did not want to admit that the dough curdled in my stomach, and sat there like a lump of concrete.

I mean, for goodness' *sake.* It wasn't as though we would never be able to go Home again. *Temporary, Ves,* I reminded myself.

And we still had Milady's chocolate pot.

'Are we thrifty?' I said, casting an eye over the table-top. It was littered with cups and teapots and plates of food, some eaten, some not. It hadn't been an inexpensive repast.

'Not the slightest bit, but it's all I can think of.'

'The Thunderstruck Three,' suggested Jay.

'It would do for now, but we will only be briefly Thunderstruck. We need something more lasting.'

Jay blinked at me. 'Why?'

'Because it's empowering. Wouldn't you rather be *The Thrilling Three* than *The Tremulous Trio*?'

'The Throwaway Three,' said Jay, and stirred his half-cup of coffee.

'Gloomy.'

'I am, a bit.'

'Right, we need to snap out of this.' I sat up straight. 'I know it's going to be hard to manage without Home, and all our friends at the Society, and Milady, and regular hot chocolate, and the first-floor common room, and the waypoint in the cellar, and the cafeteria, and Orlando's genius inventions, and your sister, and the pup, and Rob and Miranda and Val—'

'Not Rob,' interrupted Zareen. 'Milady said he'd probably catch up with us here and there, remember?'

Right. While Jay, Zareen and I had been assigned the role of disenfranchised ex-employees out to found our own rival organisation, Rob had been cast as the eternally-on-the-fence chap who couldn't make up his mind between loyalty to the Society and following the bold new direction laid down by the Thrilling Three. Which gave him an excuse to sometimes come help us out, and that was nice, but the list of things we would have to manage without went on and on in my head.

Focus, Ves.

'We can do this,' I said, opting for the short version of my little pep talk.

'Do what, exactly?' said Jay. 'I am not so experienced with Milady's double-speak as you are. One minute she was telling us *not*, under *any circumstances,* to investigate the Starstone Spire or the time-travel or the Redclovers any further and the next we're out on our ear with a mystifying carte-blanche to do anything we like.'

'We're supposed to understand that "anything we like" in this context consists of all of the things Milady had just told us not to do,' I said. 'Her hands are tied, see. She has to toe the Hidden Ministry's line, at least on the surface, and that's especially true with people like Lord Garrogin around.' Garrogin was a rare Truthseeker. That meant he knew when people were lying. He was powerful in other ways, too; not someone Milady wanted to get on the wrong side of.

'Then why not just do as she's told?'

'Jay. You cannot be serious.'

He gave me the wide-eyed, solemn look of a man who's never been more serious in the whole course of his life. 'She was right about the dangers of time-travel. If it was ever possible, the world's better off not knowing.'

'You might be right,' I conceded. 'But while we fine, law-abiding folk might be satisfied with that answer, do you think Ancestria Magicka will?'

'Doesn't have to be our problem.'

'The great thing about the Famous Five and the Secret Seven was, they never said things like that.'

'And if they'd existed in the real world, none of them would ever have reached adulthood.'

It was hard to argue with that, since I had sometimes privately thought the same thing. 'Jay,' I said instead. 'We are not going to die.'

He smiled a little at that. 'Hopefully not. We will, however, get ourselves into a lot of trouble.'

'Productive trouble.' There! Already a chance to use it.

I thought he looked ready with another litany of objections, but instead he sat up a bit, ran his hands through his thick, dark hair and nodded once. 'No use worrying, either way. The sooner we finish this up, the sooner we can go Home.'

Zareen rolled her eyes in his general direction. 'Glad you're on board after all, Negative Nancy.'

Jay cast her a look of intense annoyance. 'I'll let that pass.'

'Good show. Well then, chums, what's the objective?' Zareen put her phone away and sat looking expectantly at me.

'Er,' I said. 'When's our meeting with George again?'

'*My* meeting with George.'

'Right. That's what I said.'

'Seven-thirty at the Cupboard.' The Broom Cupboard was our favourite pub.

'You couldn't just call him?' said Jay.

'I could. But it's better to talk to him in person.'

'Why?'

Zareen smiled enigmatically. 'You'll see.'

If I suspected that Zareen's strategy was not wholly unrelated to the fetching new arrangement of her green-streaked hair and the unusually stunning black dress she was wearing, I decided to keep these observations to myself.

'All right,' I said. 'So George Mercer is our contact at Ancestria Magicka. Zareen is in charge of pumping him for information. We want to know everything they've found out about the spire, about the possibly time-travelling Redclover brothers, about the perambulating Greyer cottage, about the Dappledok pups, and about time-travel overall.'

'Sure,' said Zareen affably. 'I'll just put together a quick twenty-question questionnaire. Do you think he'd prefer multiple choice answers or free-form?'

'I realise it won't be easy,' I said.

Zareen grunted.

'Just do the best you can. At this point, any new information would be helpful.'

Zareen saluted. 'And what are you two going to do?'

'I've sent a message to Baron Alban.' I eyed Jay nervously as I said this. I was never sure how well he and the Baron got along. 'The Troll Courts have always been a repository for rare, sensitive or obscure information and I'd like to know what they've got on all of the above. After all, if this stuff is on record somewhere... well, if I can infiltrate the Court, so can Ancestria Magicka. And they probably have.'

'Cool,' said Zareen. 'Then we can be the Fabulous Four.'

'Hasn't that already been used somewhere?'

'Who cares?'

Good point.

Jay had said nothing. He sipped coffee and stared into space and I wondered if he was listening at all.

'Jay?' I said.

'Sorry. Right.' He blinked a couple of times, and his eyes narrowed in thought. 'I think we should go back to the Striding Spire.'

'It's probably crawling with Ministry agents by now,' I objected.

'It will be for a day or two, but they won't camp out there forever. They'll take the books away, and anything else deemed to be of interest or value, and then leave it alone.'

'So what would be the benefit of our going there, if there's nothing left?'

'Who knows.' Jay said this as though he, for one, might, but nothing more was forthcoming.

'You aren't going to tell me, are you?'

'Not until I have something concrete to share.'

'Fine.' I got out a notebook and wrote at the top: *Three Go Rogue.* Underneath this I added a to-do list. It read: *Talk to G. Mercer. Interrogate the Baron. Take over the spire.*

'Take over the spire?' Jay echoed. 'I didn't say anything about that.'

'No, but I did. If we're "founding" our own "rival organisation" then we'll need a headquarters, and what could be better than a four-hundred-year-old spire with a history of creative perambulation?'

'It's too small.'

'There are only three of us.'

'At the moment there are, but a new organisation will begin with recruitment. And how are we going to get there?'

'I thought we'd fly.'

'By chair?'

'Unicorn.'

Jay's objections, apparently, were satisfied, for he sat back with a shrug. Or perhaps he had just given up on me. 'You forgot to mention the sparkles.'

I couldn't suppress a faint blush. He was right; I had omitted to mention the fact that the spire was also the Starstone Spire, and it shone gloriously blue at twilight. My not listing this fact among the building's assets didn't in fact mean that I wasn't influenced by it.

Jay may only have known me for a couple of months, but he was rapidly getting my measure.

My phone rang, saving me from the trouble of answering Jay. It was the Baron. 'Hi,' I said.

'What's Wicked Little Miss Ves up to now?' He had such a deliciously low, treacly voice.

'Adventuring,' I told him brightly.

'Without Milady's sanction? I hear you've quit.'

'You hear correctly.' I wasted no time feeling surprised at how quickly he had heard this news. Gossip travels at light-speed.

'I don't believe it for a second.'

'But it's true!' I protested.

'Mm. What are you up to?'

'As it happens, I do need your help.' I said this in my most winning tones.

'It's lucky I happened to be passing, then, isn't it?' And the door of the tea-room swung open to reveal the Baron's tall, muscular frame, outlined against the lambent morning sun. He gave me a cute little salute as he approached, and made a more graceful bow to Jay and Zareen. He was wearing a very sharp, very good blue suit, bang up to date in style. The effect was devastating.

'Milord,' said Jay. 'What a surprise.' It struck me that there was a trace of suspicion on Jay's face, which I hoped the Baron had not also noticed. It was soon gone.

I pulled up a fourth chair. 'Earl Grey?' I said to the Baron.

'Please. And one of those cheesecake slices.'

'I thought you didn't like cheesecake.'

'It isn't for me, it's for you.' He smiled apologetically. 'I've got some bad news, I'm afraid.'

2

'HOME'S BURNT DOWN?' I said, as the Baron took a seat next to me.

He gave me a strange look. 'No, of course it hasn't.'

Hm. What else might rank as bad news in Baron Alban's world?

'Ancestria Magicka has taken over the Hidden Ministry,' suggested Jay.

Alban did not disclaim this idea as emphatically as I would have liked. He thought for a moment, and then said: 'Not to my knowledge.' An unspoken *yet* seemed to hover in the air.

'Stop guessing,' said Zareen. 'Let the man speak.'

The Baron tipped an imaginary hat in her general direction. 'It's Lord Garrogin,' he said. 'He's back at Court.' He looked intently at me, and then at Jay. 'Why on earth did you two tell him so much?'

'Just us two?' I protested. 'Zareen was grilled for ages.'

Zareen rolled her eyes. 'I was interrogated at length because I *wouldn't* tell him things.'

Oh.

I gave a cough. 'What did we tell him that's bad news?'

'News of your defection from the Society reached the Court late last night. Garrogin professed himself astonished. It seems the pair of you rattled on at length about your loyalty to the Society and your total lack of interest in working anywhere else.' The Baron sat back as his tea was presented to him by a smiling waitress. When she had gone, he slid the plate of cheesecake in my direction and continued: 'As a Truthseeker he's uniquely qualified to detect the perfect sincerity of everything you said, and it therefore seemed odd to him that you've suddenly broken with Milady.'

I took a spoonful of cheesecake, and savoured a mouthful of syrupy-sweet strawberry while I considered my response. 'Crap,' I said at last.

'Perhaps it won't matter,' said Jay optimistically. 'Do we need to care what they think at the Troll Court?'

'Maybe not,' conceded the Baron. 'But who are you trying to fool?'

'The Ministry, for the most part.'

I put in, 'And any other organisation with the authority to frown upon our delving into forbidden topics.'

'Like, for example, the Troll Court?' said Zareen, with withering sarcasm.

'They have no authority over *us*,' insisted Jay.

'No, but they can make plenty of trouble for us anyway.'

'It's a problem,' said the Baron. 'Because I can't really contradict Garrogin's assessment of the situation. Ves is known for her unshakeable loyalty to the Society, and anyway he's a bloody Truthseeker. People believe him. The best thing I can think of to say in your support is that it must've been something very serious to prompt you to leave, and that naturally leads to one question: *like what?*'

I might think the Hidden Ministry was wrong to put a total ban on all investigation into the arena of time-travel, but they were quite right to keep the subject quiet. We didn't need any more bright sparks like Ancestria Magicka armed with those kinds of prospects. If they wouldn't appoint a task-force to take care of the matter, well, we'd appointed ourselves. But we in no way wanted gossip spreading far and wide as to what we might be getting up to.

'So we need a cover story?' I said. 'Some other dark and dangerous thing we might have considered it worth leaving the Society for?'

'Like what?' said Alban, with a twinkle, and he was right because I could think of nothing.

Even if I could, the moment we ran into Garrogin again that particular game would be up. He'd catch us in a lie. And he'd seemed certain he would encounter us again...

...which was an interesting point. Why had he felt that way?

Baron Alban shrugged, and took a long swallow of tea. 'I don't know what the solution is. I thought it wise to warn you. For the moment, do your best to stay out of Garrogin's way?'

'Assuredly,' I murmured. As long as he stayed at the Court, that shouldn't be too hard.

'And be careful who you trust.' The Baron said this with uncharacteristic hesitation, as though reluctant to speak. 'Back Home, I mean.'

That brought a dark frown to Jay's brow, and I could not suppress a sigh. He was right, of course, and we'd known it all along. But it hurt to have to hear it spoken aloud. We knew there was a traitor at Home, and as yet, we still had no idea who it was. As far as the rest of the Society was concerned, Milady's story of our departure had to be the truth. We couldn't risk confiding in anybody else, with the probable exception of Rob.

'Why did Garrogin fail?' said Jay after a moment. 'He spoke to everyone at Home, and it's supposed to be impossible to fool a Truthseeker.'

'So they say,' said Zareen. 'But how many of them are there, now? We're mostly working with legends of the Truthseekers of old, and you know how those kinds of tales can get exaggerated.'

'Yes,' I said. 'And also, if arts like Waymastery have declined in power down the ages, might not the same be true of arts like Truthseeking? Perhaps Garrogin just isn't as good at it as his predecessors were.'

'Both good points,' said Alban. 'But there's one other possibility.'

'He does know who's betrayed us,' said Jay. 'But he's a traitor too.'

Jay seemed to be getting awfully suspicious-minded. But the Baron, to my dismay, was nodding. 'It is possible that he knows very well who your traitor is, and has always known. But if he's also in the pay of whoever's bought off your mysterious colleague, then he'd obey an order to conceal that information.'

'Damnit,' I said with a sigh, slouching in my chair. I did not like this at all. Suspicion and paranoia proliferating by the day, mysterious dangers around every corner, an inability to trust one's fellows combined with the necessity of lying to them... it was not my style. I liked openness and co-operation and goodwill.

A pox on Ancestria Magicka.

Then again, if they did contrive to learn the secrets of time-travel, a pox they would most likely have. Smallpox, perhaps, or even the Great Pox itself — syphilis.

Which reminded me. 'Dear Alban,' I began, with my best smile.

'Yes?' He did not look quite as buttered-up as I was hoping. The look he directed at me was more suspicious than charmed.

I fluttered my eyelashes, just a bit. No change.

Curse it.

'I've some questions,' I said more briskly, abandoning all hope of sweet-talking the information out of him.

He folded his muscular arms. 'No,' he said.

'No?'

'No, the Court has no secret information about travelling through time via Waymastery.'

'Damn. How about the Redclovers of Dappledok Dell?'

'Which ones?'

'The interesting ones. Melmidoc and Drystan, of the Striding Spire.' If our suspicions proved correct, these two spriggans had jaunted around in time quite at their leisure, by way of that sparkly spire I was just talking about.

'I don't know,' said Alban. 'I can check the libraries.'

'Lovely. And Ancestria Magicka?'

The Baron conceded to uncross his arms. His tea cup was empty. I offered him a forkful of cheesecake but fortunately this was spurned. 'Probably we know about as much as you do,' he said. 'It's a fairly new organisation, less than two years old. Extremely rich, though no one seems to know where their funds are coming from. Aggressive, mercenary, and sometimes dangerous. I hope you aren't planning to take them for your role-model.'

'But we are,' said Zareen. 'They're perfect. Unscrupulous, uncompromising, and working in mysterious ways. We don't have funders, so we'll have to adopt a similarly enigmatic attitude on that score. And we're plenty unscrupulous enough to investigate the spire in spite of the Ministry's strict orders not to.'

Unscrupulous. A wonderful word. 'Not a single scrup between us,' I agreed, with a big smile.

Jay looked faintly ill.

The Baron waved a hand in a *whatever* gesture, and stood up. 'Must go,' he said, then paused, and withdrew a sheet of paper from an inside jacket pocket. 'I almost forgot that.' He bowed to us, handed the paper to me with a wink, and strolled away.

It was a scan of somebody's hand-written notes, apparently the minutes of some sort of meeting. Neither the author nor the identities of the attendees were specified, but the contents were highly interesting. I read it quickly, and handed it off to Jay.

Zareen raised her eyebrows.

'Seems there've been a few reported sightings of disappearing buildings made to the Court this year,' I said. 'One of them sounds like the Greyer cottage, but there are others.'

Zareen snatched the paper from Jay and devoured its contents in hungry silence. 'I'd heard nothing of these,' she said when she'd finished. 'Though I thought I'd dug through pretty much everything.'

'The Troll Court thrives on mystery.'

Jay retrieved the paper and studied it more closely. 'The most recent of these sightings was last week.'

'Which one was that?' I asked.

'Eighteenth-century farm house, in the Cotswolds. Observed vanishing into the mists on the edge of the village of Owlpen.' He collected his phone from a pocket and after a moment's work added: 'Which is only a couple of miles from the Owlcote Troll Enclave.'

'George was in Gloucestershire recently,' said Zareen. 'Stroud area. Wouldn't say why.'

'I'm guessing this is why,' said Jay.

'Excellent.' Zareen gave the satisfied smile of a spider about to devour a particularly plump fly. 'I'll ask him about it.'

WE CHECKED OURSELVES INTO a B&B for a couple of nights. There is one in the vicinity of Home called, for reasons unknown, the Scarlet Courtyard. The proprietors are both witches, so they're tolerant of our sort. Mrs. Amberstone is about eighty years old but unbelievably spry. I can't get her to tell me what dark magic makes that possible.

'I've got a coffee cake in the oven,' she informed me as she showed me to my room, a cosy little space under the eaves with a sloping dormer window.

'I love you,' I said with total sincerity.

She winked at me as she withdrew.

Anyway, having spent the afternoon arguing about our various options and what we might be disposed to do about them ('The spire,' said Jay. 'The Cotswolds,' said Zareen. 'The Troll Court,' said I,) we arrived at The Cupboard shortly before seven.

'Off you go,' said Zareen silkily. She'd done all the eye-makeup and looked incredibly sultry.

'You promised!' I said.

'Actually, I remember myself saying "no".'

'She did,' confirmed Jay at my elbow.

'Then why did you let us come with you?'

'I don't mind your being in the same building. Just keep away from my table.'

I wanted to protest, but Jay grabbed my arm and steered me towards a table on the far side of the pub from Zareen's chosen spot. I wilted into a chair, disappointed.

'You don't seriously want to play gooseberry on Zareen's date?' Jay said, his expressive eyebrows going up.

'Is it a date?' I craned my neck to catch a glimpse of Zareen across the crowded room. 'She hardly sees him.'

'If I showed up for dinner and found all that waiting for me, I'd definitely call it a date.' He inclined his head in Zareen's direction as he uttered the word *that*, and I realised he meant the dress and the up-do and the eye-makeup.

'She's just trying to impress him so he'll talk.'

'Yes,' Jay agreed. 'By taking him on a date.'

I wondered how far Zareen's interest in George Mercer really went. Was she just being manipulative, or did she really like him? She was as enigmatic as the Troll Court.

The door opened then, and George Mercer came in. He wore a dark blazer over a t-shirt, his unruly brown hair artfully wind-swept. I hadn't taken much note of his physical characteristics before, as the first time we'd met he had been trying to knock me off my airborne pegasus and the second time he'd got straight into a fight with Jay. But now I noticed his height — at least 6'2". He was well-built, too, and good-looking in a rugged sort of way. I could see why Zareen had kept in touch.

So intent was I upon my scrutiny of his personal charms that I failed to notice he was not alone. By the time this fact had registered with me, Katalin Pataki was halfway across the pub and heading straight for our table.

'Curse it,' I muttered. 'What's she doing here?'

3

THERE ARE DEFINITELY PEOPLE I'm fonder of than Katalin Pataki. It isn't just that she happens to belong to the enemy. She also has a lamentable way of making me feel just a touch inferior. She's about a foot taller than me, with the long, sleek look of a supermodel. Why should that make me feel deficient? Well, it shouldn't. Apart from the practical advantage of being able to reach the top shelves in the cupboard without fetching a step, there is no real superiority to being taller.

Such is the folly of womankind.

Mind you, I say that but I'd noticed Jay eyeing the bulky figure of George Mercer as he came in, and his face registered the same kind of scowling irritation with which I beheld Katalin Pataki. So I'll amend that.

Such is the folly of humankind.

Anyway, Katalin waltzed up to our table with her slinky supermodel stride and stood looking down at Jay and me. She said nothing.

'Yes?' I said after a while.

She still said nothing, and I realised it wasn't me she was surveying so much as Jay. And Jay was meeting that stare with no sign of discomfort.

Well. Jay may not be half muscle, like Mercer, but he's got all that black windswept hair and those cheekbones, and with that black leather jacket he always wears there's a touch of the roguish about him. I began to wonder whether Ancestria Magicka's pursuit of him (by way of Katalin) was about more than just his juicy Waymastery skills.

'How can we help you?' said Jay, and to my irritation that prompted a half-smile and, at last, a response.

I refuse to admit that the looming-over-us-without-speaking thing was in any way intimidating.

'What are you doing on Saturday night?' she said.

Oh, please. If she must ask Jay on a date, did she have to do it right in front of my nose? As though I didn't even exist! The cheek.

To my secret relief, Jay did not have the flattered look of a man delighted to accept. His eyes narrowed, and he said with scepticism: 'What would you like us to be doing on Saturday night?' I liked the *us* in that sentence.

Katalin produced cards. Not business cards but lovely invitation cards on thick creamy paper. There was even a flash of gold gilding as she presented them to us — one each.

I examined mine in silence.

Ancestria Magicka's Summer Ball, it said, amid the usual flourishings and faff. *Ashdown Castle, Saturday 13th of May.*

If I wanted to be picky I might note that referring to the 13th of May as summer was a touch optimistic. This is Britain, after all. But that aside: what?

'Why?' said Jay, perfectly expressing my own feelings in that one syllable.

'You'll see,' she said mysteriously, and walked away.

Hm.

I exchanged a raised-eyebrow look with Jay. 'Apparently they're ready to stop hiding their HQ,' I noted.

Jay had laid his invitation on the table and sat frowning at it. 'Big event,' he said. 'And if they're inviting the enemy then they're up to something.'

'Declaration of war?'

'Maybe not quite that, but something of the kind. Taking their place on the game board, so to speak.'

I tucked my card away in my handbag. 'We'll go.'

'Definitely.'

I watched as Katalin made her way over to George and Zareen's table and repeated the procedure, though this time she only produced a card for Zareen. As a member of Ancestria Magicka, I supposed, George needed no separate invitation.

Zareen's brows went up. She said something to Katalin, but we were too far away from their table and there were too many chatty diners in between for me to hear what she was saying. Katalin's response was equally lost.

Away went Ms. Katalin Pataki, and Zareen fell into conversation with George. None of which I could hear either. I sat chafing, chewing a fingernail.

'You know,' said Jay conversationally, 'it's customary to look at your date once in a while.'

My head swivelled. 'This isn't a date!'

'No. But if you want people to think we are here for normal reasons, like, say, to have dinner and talk to one another, then stop staring fixedly at Mercer.'

He had a point, though I suspected the note of grumpiness I detected in his tone was prompted by something else. 'Sorry,' I said as graciously as I could.

Jay offered me a chip, the biggest one on his plate, which I took to mean I was forgiven. I ate it in some abstraction, for I was busy casting a charm. Only a small one, I swear. It was a charm to bring far voices near, and a busy pub was not the best place to try it, for of course it brought *all* the far voices near and for a moment I was deafened. It took a little effort to sort through all that chatter and focus on the voices of Zareen and George, during which period I stared through Jay's face, glassy-eyed.

'Well, whatever the reason for it I'm always up for a good shindig,' said Zareen clearly.

'Want to go with me?' That must have been Mercer.

'Ves,' said Jay.

'I'd be delighted,' said Zareen, and I pictured her smile.

'Great,' said Mercer, and then added smoothly: 'Where do I pick you up?'

'*Ves*,' said Jay.

'Moment.' That sounded like a probing question from Mercer, and I didn't want to miss Zar's reply.

'I'll find my way,' she said.

'You've been to Ashdown before,' said Mercer.

'Mm,' said Zareen. 'What, you couldn't afford a castle that wasn't derelict?'

'It's not entirely derelict,' objected Mercer. 'Parts of it are sound, and we'll restore the rest.'

'Still, your lot clearly doesn't lack for money. I'd have thought you would go for something better. Castle Howard, say, or Harewood House.'

'The minute they go up for sale, we'll be first in line,' said Mercer tartly. 'Until that day, we'll have to make do with Ashdown.'

Not a bad answer, for he was right: properties large enough to house an organisation of Ancestria Magicka's size were not plentiful, not if one wanted a historic place. But Zar was onto something interesting, for why did they want a historic place? So much so that it was worth buying a house half fallen down?

'You're listening in, aren't you?' said Jay in disgust.

'Shh,' I whispered.

He stared at me, brows lowered, eyes narrowed. I expected further objections from him — something along the lines of *you can't eavesdrop on somebody else's date!* — but actually he just said: 'Fine. Are you hearing anything good?'

So I began to relay everything I heard to Jay, which to nearby diners probably resembled something vaguely like dinner conversation.

Mercer said: 'How did the Society come by your house, anyway? Got any tips for us?' He said it lightly, as though it were a joke. It could easily have passed as such.

'No idea,' said Zareen, equally lightly. 'Well before my time.'

'What, aren't there stories?' Mercer laughed. 'That I cannot believe.'

'All kinds of stories — at least six for every event. Milady spreads them herself. I think it amuses her to mess with us.'

Good move, Zar, I thought silently. If there was still a traitor at Home feeding rumours to Ancestria Magicka, perhaps that would sow some doubt.

'She sounds difficult,' said Mercer.

'Terribly, but we love her.'

'Right.' Mercer's voice was sceptical. 'So you walked out on her.'

Zar waved this off with admirable insouciance. 'Sometimes it's necessary to part ways with those we love. This is important.'

'This?'

Zar lowered her voice. 'You know. Wester and the Greyer cottage. The pups. What happened to the Redclover brothers. All of it.'

George Mercer sat back in his chair, scrutinising Zareen with an unreadable look.

'You're staring again,' said Jay, and I slumped back with a sigh. 'Worst sleuth ever,' he added, though his lips twitched in a smile.

I rolled my eyes at him.

Mercer was speaking again. 'What am I doing here, Zar?'

'Having dinner with me.' I could hear the bright smile in her voice as she said it.

'To what end? It's been years since you and me, and all of a sudden you want to have dinner? I don't buy it.'

'Quite right.' Zareen was suddenly brisk. I heard a clatter of cutlery as she, presumably, set aside her plate. 'I've come with an offer.'

'Oh?'

'A pact. We have the same goals, George. Ves and Jay and I, we know what the Waymasters of old used to be able to do. The Redclover brothers at least, and possibly others besides. The Ministry might be intent on hushing it up but I know that Ancestria Magicka is determined to discover the whole truth — and so are we. Help us, and we'll help you.'

I saw my own horror reflected in Jay's dark eyes, for *that* certainly had not been part of the plan. Just what did Zareen think she was doing?

4

'I'M BUILDING ALLIANCES,' SAID Zareen a little later, once George Mercer had gone. 'Which is the first thing anybody in our situation would do. What can we expect to achieve with exactly three people?'

Jay was not impressed. 'You couldn't have consulted us about this brilliant plan?'

Zareen wasn't impressed either. 'You couldn't have chosen a different pub to have dinner? Or did you think George couldn't see you sitting there?'

Jay shot me a look, which I interpreted to mean it was all my fault.

'Mercer was never going to believe you just wanted to see him, whether we were there or not,' I said, in my own defence.

'Quite,' said Zareen shortly. 'And I wanted to distract him. Note all those questions he was asking?' She smiled mirthlessly. 'You *were* listening?'

'We were,' I said. 'And I did.'

'If Katalin knew he was with me, so did his superiors. He was sent to bleed me for information, just as I was trying to bleed him. Well, he can take that snippet of gossip back with him and we'll see what they do.'

'They'll agree,' I said. 'It's the perfect way to keep tabs on us.'

'Supposing they want to,' said Jay.

'Why wouldn't they?'

'Why would they?' Jay countered. 'As Zareen has just pointed out, there are exactly three of us. Without the Society at our backs, what can we be expected to achieve that would put Ancestria Magicka in a tizz?'

'We may be only three, but we get results,' I objected. 'Who was it that found out about the Greyer cottage?'

'They did. We may have found it first, but only by about twenty-five minutes — and they were on the trail well before we knew anything about it.'

That was, annoyingly, true. 'Well then, the Redclover brothers and the spire. We did that on our own.'

Jay patted me on the shoulder. 'I'm sure they're quaking in their boots.'

George Mercer had left with a promise to think over Zareen's offer, which Zar had interpreted to mean "receive instruction from his bosses", whoever they were. The rest of their conversation had yielded very little, for they'd put each other on guard by then, and they were both skilled conversational fencers. Zar had dropped lots of intriguing, but not very informative, hints about our recent discoveries, all of which Mercer had failed to follow up on — which might mean that he already knew all about them, or merely that he was too clever to take the bait. Zar treated his various light-hearted queries, jokes and remarks in the same fashion. She hadn't been able to draw him on the subject of his trip to Gloucestershire, either. He'd claimed to have gone there on a mundane errand — picking up a new recruit. It could have been true.

I was privately horrified at the idea of our developing a close association with George Mercer, or anybody else from Ancestria Magicka. It's difficult to pretend to help somebody without actually doing anything useful for them. Sooner or later you do actually have to help, and how was that going to pan out? I didn't want to help them. Neither did Jay. They'd take anything we gave them and find a way to do something terrible with it, and there was no guarantee that we'd glean anything of much use in return.

But Zar was serene. I hoped fervently that she knew what she was doing.

WE SPENT AN UNEVENTFUL night at The Scarlet Court-yard. No one came to spy on us, no one tried to kidnap us, nothing went mysteriously missing... all told it was a bit disappointing. We awoke in the morning feeling a touch let down.

That lasted until I was approximately halfway through a plate of eggs and toast in Mrs. Amberstone's pretty east-facing morning room. I received a call.

'It's Rob,' I said to Zareen and Jay as I picked it up. 'The bonds of the Society have begun to chafe and you're ready to join us?' I said into the phone.

'Not just yet,' said Rob in his deep, calm voice. 'But I'm seriously thinking about it, Ves.'

'I could be very persuasive.' And I might, too. For all that I'd argued, I privately agreed just a bit with Jay: the three of us could use some help.

'This I know, to my cost. Any news for me?'

I relayed Zareen's surprise manoeuvre regarding George Mercer.

'Keep your enemies close,' remarked Rob.

'There's such a thing as too close.'

'So there is. Do you want my news?'

I desperately did. Rob talked for a couple of minutes and then rang off, with a solemn promise to send me all further developments as soon as they arose.

'There's been an outbreak of Dappledok pups,' I told my trusty companions, and began hastily scooping up the remains of my breakfast. 'Three spotted at different places around England. Two of them popped up in magicker communities — Rob's sending details — but one's been seen scurrying around in the Cotswolds.'

'That house,' said Jay.

I nodded, my mouth full of toast.

'Right.' He stood up. 'We're going.'

I took the toast with me, and followed.

'Where the bloody hell are they coming from?' said Zareen.

I didn't have the slightest idea either, but it was definitely time to find out.

Jay whisked us away to Gloucestershire, and I soon developed the feeling that I might never want to leave again. We came out in a featureless field, notably devoid of visible henge — 'Stones are gone, still works,' said Jay briefly in answer to our puzzled faces — and set off in the direction of habitation.

And habitation proved to be a drippingly gorgeous Tudor manor set among wooded emerald hills, the latter dotted about with the kinds of places people mean when they talk of the English country cottage. Pure idyll. The walk to Owlpen village took us only a few minutes, but I would've been happy had it taken an hour. Golden morning sunshine drenched everything around us, making the greenery glow with a light almost magical, and the air smelled fresh in the way that only spring can bring.

There isn't much left of the village, though there are signs that it used to be rather larger. Jay led us to a spot some thirty feet from the narrow village road, hidden from the few scattered stone houses that made up the settlement. 'The vanishing house was seen around here,' he said, stamping lightly on the grassy earth with one booted foot.

A swift look around confirmed that no, there really wasn't an eighteenth-century farmhouse loitering in the bushes. 'It always appears in the same place?'

'So say the reports. But they aren't always very specific. You know the kind of thing. "Well, it was near the gate into that field that used to belong to Farmer Wells — the one with the twisted oak at the north-west corner? Where Marjorie fell and broke her leg last winter." And it's no use asking which of several possible fields they're referring to, or what "near" means anyway.' Jay walked as he talked, hands in the pockets of his jacket, moving in ever-widening circles.

Zareen and I joined in, watching for any sign of a two-hundred-year-old building hidden among the trees, or crouched behind a rambling hedgerow.

'Should be anywhere within about a mile's radius...' said Jay, then stopped. 'Aha. Farmhouse ahoy, suitably incongruous. Looks like flint?'

I hurried to catch up with him. 'That is indeed flint,' I said, which is relevant, I promise. Flint stones are not a popular building material in those parts of the country supplied with better options, like limestone, or good clay for bricks. Flint properties are usually found in East Anglia, which has a lot of flint and not much of anything else. So I'd wager this farmhouse originated from somewhere nearer Norwich than Stroud.

'Good work, men,' I murmured.

'Thank you, ma'am.' Jay tipped an imaginary hat to me, and off we went.

'Wait,' I said, stopping. 'Where's Zar?'

Jay gave a cursory look around. 'Doubtless off getting into mischief. She'll catch up.'

Knowing Zareen, that was fair enough.

The farmhouse had parked itself on the edge of a tiny copse of ash and birch trees. It looked innocuous enough, flint excepted, and quite as though it could almost belong there. The place had not been well maintained, for parts of the walls were crumbling, chunks of flint having dropped out long ago, and the white paint adorning the sash windows was peeling. Jay and I approached cautiously, half-expecting to be challenged, but the morning air was breathlessly still and nothing moved.

'I think I'll try your trick,' said Jay, and walked up to the blue-painted front door. A dull brass knocker hung there; Jay rapped loudly with it several times.

Nothing stirred.

'Hello?' called Jay, and when that, too, was productive of nothing he raised his voice still further. 'Come on! There must be someone in residence, even if you aren't alive. Someone of a Waymasterly persuasion, probably long dead, wrapped around this house like a bad smell... aha.' Rudeness apparently had its benefits, for the heavy blue door creaked open and swung ponderously inward.

'I beg your pardon?' said a cool, female voice. Refined. She had undoubtedly been gentry when she was alive.

'Just trying to get your attention,' said Jay, with one of his more charming smiles. I wondered if it would still work on someone who'd been a house for longer than she'd been a woman.

Apparently it did, for the door opened a bit wider. 'Do you play whist?' said the house.

'No, but I'm sure you could teach me.' Jay paused upon the doorstep. 'Whom do I have the honour of addressing?'

The door swung back and forth a bit, creaking. 'Mellicent Makepeace, of the Newmarket Makepeaces,' she said. The voice had definitely warmed. 'And who calls upon me?'

'Jay Patel, of the Nottingham Patels.' Jay peered cautiously through the half-open door.

'A pleasure, Mr. Patel,' said Mellicent, and the door swung wide again. 'I am perfectly safe, I can assure you. There is no one home this morning. I am quite alone.'

'Then you must be lonely,' said Jay.

'I am!' The words emerged as a forlorn wail. 'Will you keep me company?'

'For a little while, Miss Makepeace. I believe you may be able to help me with something.'

I'd joined Jay at the door by this time, but I said nothing, preferring not to interrupt his rapport with little Miss Makepeace. Jay leaned towards me and whispered, 'Wait here a minute?'

I opened my mouth to ask why I was to be left languishing on the doorstep but Jay had already gone, darting through the door before I could utter more than two syllables.

To my dismay, the blue door shut crisply behind him.

'Miss Makepeace?' I called.

Either I did not have Jay's charm or she was unresponsive to my particular brand of it, for there came no reply.

I began to have a bad feeling.

This feeling quadrupled when a tremor ran through the ground beneath my feet, and all the misshapen flintstones in the farmhouse's walls rattled. I jumped back instinctively. Mist rose up in a thick, billowing cloud, obscuring the lower half of the house — and then the whole thing was gone, leaving the copse of youthful ash trees swaying dreamily in the winds of its passage.

I stared numbly at the spot where the farmhouse had been.

'Jay?' I called.

Of course, there was no reply.

5

'So,' I said, as Zareen strolled up a few moments later. 'I've lost Jay.' I had tried three times to call him, but he hadn't answered.

'Lost, how?' she said. 'Or do I mean, how lost?'

'I'd say he's the kind of lost that nightmares are made of, and I lost him because I let him go into Little Miss Makepeace's creepy farmhouse alone.'

'And she made off with him?'

'Correct.'

'Why did you let him go in alone?'

'Because he told me to wait.'

'And you obeyed?' Zareen was incredulous.

'For about three seconds, which turned out to be long enough.'

Zareen shrugged, splendidly unconcerned about Jay's abrupt disappearance. 'All part of the plan, most likely. Do you want to know what I found?'

'Is it something exciting?'

'Extremely.' Zareen's plum-painted lips wore a huge, satisfied smile.

But her revelation was forestalled, because we both became aware of a rustling noise emanating from somewhere among the trees where the house had so lately stood. It sounded like an animal rooting about among the bushes — a dog, I might have said, and was proved right moments later when a dog duly appeared. A small specimen, it had jaunty yellowish fur, an enormous nose (presently glued to the ground) and a tiny horn protruding from its forehead.

'Oh, there are more,' said Zareen, and went forward to meet the pup. Being a friendly sort, it greeted her with a cheery wave of its tail, though it did not seem disposed to lift its nose from the ground.

Zareen scooped it up, and held its little wriggling body close to her chest. 'I saw two back that way,' she said, pointing somewhere behind me with her chin. 'So, three? Reckon there are more?'

'Oh, my giddy aunt,' I groaned. 'Three more of the blighters?'

'Wouldn't be surprised if there are more than three. Miranda's going to die of joy.'

'And everyone else is going to run for the hills, taking their valuables with them.' My thoughts were in a flutter with so much happening at once; I took a couple of steadying breaths, and made myself think. 'Right. Call Home, and…' I stopped. Calling Home for back-up wasn't an option anymore. 'Call Rob,' I said instead. As I spoke, I dragged open the flap of my ever-present shoulder bag and hauled out my favourite book. 'Morning, Mauf,' I greeted him.

Mauf's pages riffled in greeting. 'Good morning, Miss Vesper. How may I be of assistance?'

'Quick job for you.' I stroked the rich purple leather of his covers. He liked that, and it always put him in a helpful mood. 'That bookmark looks great,' I added, for a little flattery never hurts.

The bookmark in question, a pure silk ribbon dyed majestic gold, fluttered coquettishly. 'Why thank you, Miss Vesper. If I may say so, you made a fine choice. What an eye for textiles!'

I may have preened a bit, too. Flattery works both ways. 'You shall have another sometime,' I promised him. 'For the moment, can you tell me if you have any information about one Mellicent Makepeace, of the Newmarket Makepeaces?'

Mauf went quiet for a moment. Presumably he was searching through his… memory? Records? It was hard to tell how it worked with him. 'There was a family of that name in the Newmarket area,' he confirmed. 'Is there any particular era of interest to you?'

'Eighteenth century?'

'Ooh,' said Mauf.

'You've found something?'

The book literally wriggled with glee. 'Millie Makepeace, daughter of Mr. William Makepeace of Broneham Manor.'

'Excellent.'

'Family of only moderate wealth, I would guess, though squarely genteel. Miss Makepeace appears to have been a model citizen.'

'That's a relief.'

'Until she was hanged for murder in 1779.'

My relief turned to chagrin. 'Not *again*.'

Zareen poked her nose over my shoulder. 'Who'd she kill?'

'The cook. There had been an altercation earlier in the day, the subject being a pudding which Miss Makepeace thought improperly prepared.'

Zareen actually giggled. 'That's fantastic.'

'She killed someone over a dessert?' I spluttered. 'Zar, this madwoman has hold of Jay. This is anything but fantastic.'

'Right.' Zareen sobered. 'But she likes Jay, Ves. It's that smile. He'll have her eating out of the palm of his hand by now.'

I wasted a second or two picturing the smile in question — undeniably attractive — before I pulled myself together. 'Did you call Rob?'

'Yes, but I'm guessing you'll want to call him again now.'

I did indeed. Fortunately he picked up right away. 'If this is about the pups—' he began.

'It's not.' I rattled off an account of the latest development.

'Right,' said Rob when I'd finished. 'I'll see that this reaches Milady. Miranda's on her way to collect the pups. Have you found out where they're coming from?'

'Not as such, but I can only imagine they came from the house that's just wandered off with Jay.'

'Then Jay is well-placed to investigate and I'm sure we'll hear from him soon. There's no way you can follow the house, I suppose?'

'Not that I've yet discovered, but working on it.'

I like Rob so much. As capable of harming people as he is of healing them, he's nonetheless the most grounded person I know. Nothing ruffles him.

I stashed my phone and turned back to Mauf. 'Maufy, why is it that these house-toting Waymasters are always murderers, cut-throats and thieves?'

'*Always* would not be correct, but there is a definite pattern emerging,' Mauf agreed. 'In 1697, Roderick Vale of Bantam Cross put forward the theory that magical abilities are sometimes amplified in times of crisis. He cited several pertinent examples, of which three were convicted murderers or thieves condemned to death by hanging. They performed extraordinary feats well outside their usual capabilities, though admittedly the goal at the time was to escape hanging and there is no indication that this enhancement of their powers proved permanent. Or *would* have proved permanent if they had not actually been executed, which two of them duly were. Then in 1741, Harriet Bodkin wrote in *On the Unfortunate Matter of Dark Magicke* that committing terrible deeds had been seen to have a similar effect on what are nowadays referred to as the darker arts, or perhaps the stranger arts, and—'

'Mauf,' I interrupted him. 'I love you. Let's finish this conversation a bit later, okay?'

'Yes, ma'am.'

I hoped he was not offended. Mauf could be prickly sometimes. But if I let him really get going, he'd ramble on all day.

I returned him to his sleeping-bag in the satchel. 'So if Roderick and Miss Bodkin were correct, it's no coincidence that the likes of the Greyers and Miss Makepeace were chosen for hauling houses around. Maybe no one else had the capacity.'

'Yes, but.' Zareen was frowning. 'Waymastery has never been classified among the stranger arts, has it?'

'Perhaps terrible deeds don't only enhance the stranger powers. Maybe it works on the other arts, too.'

'Why would it?'

'Good question.' Very good question. The idea didn't seem to hold much water; I could think of several vastly powerful witches and sorcerers off the top of my head who'd never so much as squashed a spider. Nonetheless, the Greyers and John Wester and Mellicent Makepeace formed a clear pattern. If it was not that their deeds influenced their arts, what else was it about them?

'I wonder how long Millie's been cooped up in that house,' I mused aloud.

'Since her death,' said Zareen promptly. 'Like Wester. Those kinds of arts are time-sensitive. I mean, you maybe *could* dig up someone who's been dead a while, re-bury them in a new site and hope there's enough of their spirit left to harness for your nefarious purposes, but in most cases there won't be. Ancestria Magicka knows this. That's why they were after the Greyer cottage — if you want to make a fresh, new perambulatory building you need live spirits, so to speak. If Millie had been hanged and buried as normal, her spirit would either have passed on or wandered off within a few days.'

'In that case, I wonder who bound her to the house? She must be buried somewhere in there, no?'

'Right. Someone purloined her corpse, post-hanging, and sited her in the farmhouse. We'll ask her sometime.'

I thought. 'Do you suppose she went back to Newmarket?'

'To the place of her crime and subsequent execution? Doubtful. I mean, would you?'

It occurred to me that our options were severely diminished without our pet Waymaster. If Jay were here, I'd have suggested we pop down to Newmarket to check. But here we were, hundreds of miles away and with no convenient means of transport.

'Options,' I said. 'We can go to Newmarket the slow way and see if Millie's there with Jay. We can wait here a while and hope the house comes back. Or we can move on to the next thing.'

'What's the next thing?' If Zareen wasn't already best friends with that pup, she was working on it. The pup was rubbing its furry little face all over her cheek. I felt a tiny bit jealous.

'The spire,' I said. 'Jay wanted to go back there. He had some plan in mind, which being Jay he did not impart. I think I've an idea what he was up to, though.'

'Gets my vote.' Zareen spoke around a huge, soppy smile, and kissed the pup's face.

'But Jay—'

'Is a grown man. I know you feel responsible for him, but you aren't. He can handle himself.'

She was right, but still. I called Rob again. 'Rob, about Jay. The Mellicent Makepeace house came from the Newmarket area and it might have gone back there. Can we possibly send someone to check?'

'We?' said Rob. 'I thought you three were going it alone now.'

'*Rob.*'

He laughed. 'I'll go myself. Send me the address.'

I did that, feeling better. Zareen was probably right on all points, but it still didn't sit right with me to just leave Jay to his fate. If he was at Mellicent's old village and in some kind of trouble, there was no one better than Rob to help get him out of it.

If he wasn't at Mellicent's old village, well... I had no way of finding out where else he might have been taken to.

Focus, Ves.

'Right,' I muttered, and fished my tiny syrinx pipes out of my shirt. 'Soon as someone gets here to pick up these pups, we're airborne. Where did you say the others were?'

WE ENJOYED AN ENTERTAINING time chasing down the rest of the Dappledok pups. There proved to be four, at least that we discovered, and keeping them with us was no easy task. I'd privately hoped that Mellicent might consent to return Jay while we were waiting for Miranda, but I was to be disappointed. When at last Miranda appeared with two of her kennel aides and a quartet of travel-baskets between them, there remained only an empty space where the farmhouse had previously been.

Miranda barely looked at Zareen or me. She had eyes only for the pups, and the feeling was apparently mutual, for they mobbed her at once. I told myself it was because of the treats she kept in her pockets, some of which were duly distributed as she coaxed them into the baskets. Only once all four pups were safely confined and ready to go did she focus on me. 'No further info on where they've come from, I suppose?'

'Nope.' We'd explored the area a bit more while we waited, but without turning up anything of use. 'They were most likely brought here in Mellicent's farmhouse, like the one we found at the Greyer cottage. But where they came from before that, we've no idea.'

'Jay might, though,' said Zareen.

'True.' I called him again. Still no answer.

'Well, let me know if you get hold of him,' said Miranda. She quirked a smile at the both of us and added, 'How's the rogue life treating you?'

'We're doing great!' I said enthusiastically. 'I've only called Rob about five times today, and this is the first time since at *least* this morning we've had to call in for help.'

Miranda grinned. 'You know, nothing would've stopped me from coming down here for these little chaps, but I did feel obliged to run it past Milady first. She said to give you anything you needed.'

'Did she indeed?'

'So you're rogue with Milady's official sanction? That's different.'

'You should know, Mir. Life with the Society is never simple.'

She gave me a tiny salute. 'Got it. Oh, Val sent this for you.' She drew a little book out of the pocket of her waxed jacket and handed it to me. 'And...' She rummaged for a moment, then produced a shabby-looking pamphlet for Zareen.

There was no text of any kind on the cover or the spine of my book, but the pages inside were covered in faded hand-written script. The title page read simply: *Mellicent Makepeace, 1778.*

'How the bloody hell did Val get hold of this?' I squeaked.

'Never question the Queen of the Library.' Miranda collected her two baskets, nodded to us, and retreated to her car, her aides trailing behind her. It occurred to me, distantly, that I had never seen either of them before. New recruits? I felt an odd sensation of devastation. Barely two days away from the Society and I was already out of touch.

I shook off the feeling. 'What's yours?' I said, showing Zareen the title page of my book.

She whistled. 'It's a treatise on the Stranger Arts and their connection to "dark deeds", as the author puts it. More or less what Mauf was saying. Late 1600s, anonymous.' It was bound in what looked, to my reasonably experienced eye, like human skin, which could not but make me shudder a little to behold.

My satchel was vibrating. I opened it and hauled out Mauf, who was (in his bookly fashion) spluttering with indignation. 'I've never *met* such books!' he said. 'Let me have them at once.'

Meekly, we put Mauf back in the satchel and added Val's donations. Mauf consented to settle down.

'Just as well,' I said. 'It's hard to read on horseback anyway.' I lifted my face to the wind and blew a ditty on my silver pipes. The melody rang out, bright and clear.

As ever, Adeline appeared within minutes. I probably never would understand quite how she managed it. She trotted up to me, her silvery-white coat gleaming in the sun, and nuzzled me with her velvety nose.

'I'm sorry,' I whispered. 'I don't have any chips today.'

She snorted.

'Later,' I promised.

She had brought her night-black friend with her, who walked calmly up to Zareen and stood waiting. I wasn't altogether sure that Zareen knew how to ride a horse, but I was soon reassured: she jumped nimbly onto the unicorn's back and settled there, her eyes bright. 'I've never flown by unicorn,' she told me.

I mounted up — Addie is obliging enough to lower herself a bit to help me out, seeing as I *am* rather short — and took hold of her silver harness. 'Hold tight,' I advised, and clucked my tongue to Adeline. 'To Nautilus Cove, darling!' I told her.

She broke into a gallop, her powerful wings beating in time with her stride, and we rose smoothly into the air. The fresh, spring wind enveloped me, bringing with it (somehow) the scents of honeysuckle and chocolate, and I swear a sparkling, rosy mist blew lightly past my eyes.

I do love travelling by unicorn.

6

ALL RIGHT, USUALLY I love travelling by unicorn.

I tend to assume that Addie knows her way from everywhere to anywhere, which, as it turns out, is far too much to expect of the poor girl. Also, as anyone who's ever taken more than an occasional leisurely hack across the countryside will tell you, the delights of being on horseback tend to wane after a certain point. Zareen and I made the long journey to Norfolk in a state of increasingly grim determination, wrestling with mobile navigation systems which had no idea that Nautilus Cove even existed.

I might have been ungenerous enough to curse Jay and his inconvenient absence, but that was only while I was still airborne, gritting my teeth against the surprisingly cold wind while my hair blew into my mouth and my derriere voiced vociferous complaints about its treatment at my uncaring hands. Once Addie brought us down on a quiet little slip of a beach along the Norfolk coast and we were able to dismount — and once the warmer air down there had somewhat thawed out my face — I lost all desire to eviscerate Jay and was able to remember that I was worried about him.

I checked my phone. Nothing.

Patting Addie's steaming neck, I whispered foolish compliments into her ears and promised her the biggest bag of chips she had ever seen in her life, just as soon as I made it to a chippie. She rolled her eyes at me and wandered off, her shadowy friend trotting amiably in her wake.

'Right, then,' I said, looking up and down the deserted beach. The greyish sea lapped apathetically at the rocky sand, a few clouds hung listlessly in a patchy blue sky, and behind us a cliff rose vertically to an unscaleable height. 'Addie?' I called. 'You wouldn't happen to know how to get *in*?' I cursed myself for not having paid more attention on the way out, a few days before. Riding with the baron had proved to be a distracting experience.

I had not really expected a response, but a moment later Zareen said: 'Up there!' and pointed a ways back along the beach.

Something was glittering upon the sheer cliff face. Fittingly, it shone in rainbow colours.

We went that way.

The glow was coming from a sliver of jagged crystal embedded into the otherwise drab rock. When I touched it, the colours faded, leaving it an unremarkable chunk of opaque white stone. But the world shifted around me and dissolved, and when everything stopped spinning I was on another, whiter, pearlier beach, and the sea had gone all iridescent. Nautilus Cove.

I mentally doubled Addie's upcoming chip rations.

Zareen materialised a moment later and stood smiling for a moment, taking great inhalations of the balmy air. It *did* smell rather heavenly, come to think of it — like the brightest, freshest sea air mingled with something flowery. I couldn't see any flowers, but one doesn't question things like that when one is prancing through a magickal dell. It's the way they are.

I'd had a private, lingering fear that we might return to find the Striding Spire had, somehow, gone. Stridden Off, in the way that it used to, or perhaps been somehow relocated by an indignant Ministry. But it hadn't. The clear, white beach gave way to an expanse of sleek, jade-coloured grass dotted with frondy bits (botany is not among my specialities). In the near distance the ground began a steep climb up into some rolly hills, and halfway up those was the spire. I hadn't previously had occasion to see it from this perspective, and the sight was breath-taking. So graceful a building! Tall and slender, crowned with an elegantly sloping roof (I'd seen as much as I wanted to of that part), its windows glinted gently in the sunlight and its pale walls displayed a hint of the bluish radiance that would come in with the twilight.

'The Redclovers had style,' Zareen said.

They certainly did. 'Why, then, is it abandoned out here?' I mused aloud. 'If you'd built something that lovely, why would you ever leave?'

'The passage of four hundred years is neither here nor there, I suppose?'

I strode off in the direction of the spire, my boots swishing through the crisp grass. 'Not with these people. Their bodies may have died long ago but I doubt they went far after that. I'm willing to bet that the spire had a Waymaster-in-residence, John Wester-style, for a long time, and maybe it still does.'

'So that's what Jay had in mind?'

'Yes. Especially after Millie. Wester obviously wasn't some kind of a fluke, and if there have been more of them — why not Melmidoc?'

'You saw no sign of him before?'

'He's an old man. He fell asleep over his newspaper a hundred and ten years ago, and has yet to wake up.'

Zareen grinned. 'Right, then. Let's go rattle his door handles and throw stones at the windows.'

My previous visit to the spire had been only a few days prior, but I found a much-changed building when we went inside. Rattling the doorknobs proved unnecessary, as the door was unlocked. And why not? There was nothing left in there, nothing at all. The kitchen on the ground floor was reduced to a collection of aged wooden counters, probably left in situ because they were both unlovely and (I imagined) heavy. The bright, circular room near the top which had previously held all the accoutrements of a comfortable living space was completely empty. The chairs were gone, the knick-knacks and ornaments, and above all, the books. All of them.

Someone had cleaned, for not a speck of dust floated up as Zareen and I tramped up the winding stairs. That was nice, I supposed.

'They did a thorough job,' Zar said as we stood in the doorway of the Redclover brothers' decimated library.

'I wonder why.' I was wondering that pretty hard. Taking the books I could understand, even if I was disappointed. They were a valuable resource, and were liable to be damaged if left uncared for on such remote shelves. But the furniture?

I felt that unwelcome but sadly familiar sensation of foreboding.

Jay and I made the acquaintance of Mabyn Redclover during our previous investigation of the Dappledok pups, a spriggan who was somewhere high-up in the Forbidden Magicks division of the Hidden Ministry. I blessed my forethought in making sure to secure her number, and called it.

'Ms. Redclover, Forbidden Magicks.' Mabyn's voice came crisply over the line.

'Mab. It's Ves. I'm at the spire, but nothing much else is.'

'I was going to call you this afternoon,' said Mabyn, and she sounded grim. 'The Ministry finished emptying the building day before last. There was a bloodbath over the books, as you may imagine, with strong competition from the Troll Court to secure them. In the end they split the books, but the Ministry took everything else. I've only just found out why. It's scheduled for demolition, Ves, and soon. They want it gone, no delay.'

'I thought it must be something like that,' I said. 'Any idea why?'

'None whatsoever. I've spent the whole morning trying to get an audience with the right people and I've largely failed. They won't talk to me. I was reduced to loitering in the hallways hoping to run into the Chief or Vice-Chief Ministers. Well, I did see Honoria Goodenough — that's the Vice-Chief — but she said I'm too close to the situation and wouldn't listen to me. Just because I'm a Redclover! It's not like I have any real connection to a pair of

Redclovers from four hundred years ago. I tried to argue that it's a rare and precious example of seventeenth-century magickal architecture and its starstone composition ought to be enough to secure instant and eternal protected status but she wasn't having it. Nor would she tell me why. I'm sorry, Ves. There's nothing more I can do.'

I hadn't known Mabyn for very long, but long enough to learn that it was unlike her to gabble. She was genuinely upset. 'It's all right, Mab. I'm glad you tried. Do you know when it's due to be demolished?'

'They've kept that information from me. What do they expect me to do, throw myself in front of the demolition force? It's ridiculous. But it'll be soon. As in, possibly this week. I have set something in motion which I hope will delay them, but I don't know if it can be there in time. I'm sorry, Ves.'

'Right. Don't worry, we'll fix this.' I hung up.

Zareen's face was grave as I relayed Mabyn's news, but she spoke composedly. 'That ties in with our suspicions, doesn't it? This building's completely unique and irreplaceable. If they're willing to wreck it anyway, that more or less confirms that it's been used for something they'd consider seriously questionable.'

'More than that. They think it could be used the same way again.'

Zareen was nodding emphatically. 'Jay's not the only one who thinks Melmidoc's still here.'

'Yes, but I'm wondering how he arrived at that conclusion. I was hoping for just such an outcome last time I was here, but I swear, I felt not a flicker of a presence. Does it take a Waymaster to spot another? Jay's rather discouraged that idea, but in that case, why was he in a hurry to come back?'

'I know that look.' Zareen eyed me with sour suspicion. 'You want me to do something, don't you?'

I might have been wearing the pleading eyes, at that. I hastily composed my face. 'Those Stranger Arts you aren't supposed to talk about? Could you somehow sense a spirit presence, even if it's dormant?'

'Or determined to hide from me? I don't know.' Zareen looked annoyed, for no reason I could understand. Then she sighed, and passed a hand over her eyes. It occurred to me that she was looking tired, dark shadows etched under her deep brown eyes. Her shimmery green eyeshadow did a fine job of deflecting attention from them. She hesitated, apparently struggling with herself. 'Look, Ves,' she finally said. 'The Stranger Arts — or the Weird Stuff — it's not quite like your magick. It... takes a toll. I'm not supposed to talk about it partly because I'm not supposed to use it, except at great need. And there are good reasons for that.'

'What kind of a toll?'

A deep frown clouded Zareen's brow. I almost hadn't wanted to ask, for the matter clearly troubled her. But if it was important...

'It's to do with Mauf's bright idea about the... amplifying effects of... of—' she stopped. 'Look, if all power corrupts, let's just say that some kinds of power corrupt faster than others. And the link isn't as clear-cut as Mauf, or those wannabe scholars, suggested. If I get too immersed in the weird stuff, I... it changes me. I feel a need to do some terrible things, Ves, and if I give in to them... I *will* be more powerful. Only for a short time, of course. It's like a hit of caffeine, or steroids. When it wears off, you feel as weak as a newborn kitten, and to add to the fun it's like the worst kind of withdrawal you can experience — crack is nothing to it—' She stopped again, her expression turning wary. She'd said more than she meant to.

For a moment, I was too shocked to speak. This was a glimpse into Zareen's daily life, and her past as well, that I'd never before been offered.

She (and George Mercer) had expended considerable power and effort to exorcise the spirits of the Greyers and John Wester from the Greyer cottage. After that, she'd gone quiet for twenty-four hours — I hadn't seen her, or heard anything from her. At the time, I thought nothing of it. Zareen and I were friends, but not to the extent that we talked every day, or kept tabs on each other all the time.

Now I wondered what had been going on with her during those hours of silence.

I looked at the shadows under her eyes with a new understanding.

'I didn't know,' I said at last.

Zareen shrugged. 'The School of Weird isn't just a special school for people with our abilities. It's also a kind of quarantine, a help centre, a support group and rehab all rolled into one. It needs to be.'

That also explained her enduring link with George Mercer. He understood her in ways Jay and I never could, and they must've shared so much... I resolved never to tease or poke her about that friendship ever again.

And I understood what she had not said, at least not in so many words. After her efforts at the Greyer cottage, she needed time to recover, to rebalance herself. She couldn't afford to drown in the Stranger Arts again so soon.

I remembered the way the whites of her eyes had filled in with black, and shuddered inwardly.

'Right then,' I said briskly. 'How else can we wake up Mr. Redclover?'

'Throwing stones at the windows is out?' Zareen gave a weak smile.

'If he slept through the removal of the entire contents of the building, I'd say we need something a little more potent.' I thought hard.

I came up with nothing.

'Maybe we could—' began Zareen, but the rest of her sentence was drowned out by a terrific roar that sounded from outside — somewhere close. The spire's glorious starstones shook under the force of it.

Zareen and I ran to the window, just in time to see a gout of crackling fire lance across the sky.

'That's dragon-fire!' shouted Zareen.

Another blast of fire followed seconds later, and this one hit the window. The window-frame caught and flames roared cheerfully to life, blocking the sunlight and casting dancing patterns across the floor of the tower. The reek of smoke filled my nostrils.

'Mabyn was wrong,' I said tightly. 'The demolition isn't just *this week*. It's today.'

7

'We have to get out,' I said, turning from the spire's burning window. I was halfway to the stairs before I re-alised Zareen was not following.

She stood in the centre of the room, and there was a set look to her face that I recognised. Her skin was turning bone-white, and her eyes filling with black...

'Zar!' I snapped, and ran back to her. 'No! What did you *just* say to me?'

'I *said* "times of great need", and this would be one of them.'

'Within reason. Zar, I'd love to save this building but not at your expense. Come on.' I grabbed her arm and tried to pull her, but she shook off my hand.

'All I'm doing is waking Melmidoc,' she said, and her voice turned dark and whispery. 'If he's still home. Then we'll go, I promise.'

I would have argued, but my attention was caught by the flames that licked at the window's little panes of glass. For the most part it was your regular, common-or-garden variety of fire but there was a flicker to it that seemed odd.

'Purple,' I blurted.

Zareen didn't blink.

'Hold on, Zar! I don't think this is the demolition crew after all.' I ran to the window, pulling the sleeves of my lightweight cream cardigan over my hands. It did not do much to protect my hands, so I had to work fast as I unbolted the window and shoved it wide open. At great risk to life, limb and my primrose-coloured hair (Yes, Jay, I know I'm an idiot) I stuck my head out into the fresh morning air and took in a gulping breath.

A dark, draconic shape swooped past.

'Archie!' I bellowed.

The dragon slowed, but not, as it turned out, because he had heard me. He flew in a smooth arc and swooped down upon the hapless spire once more, fire streaming from his open maw.

'*Archibald!*' I bawled. 'Just what the bloody hell do you think you're doing?!'

He heard me that time. To my relief, the stream of fire flowing from his jaws slowed to a wisp or two of flame, then stopped altogether. 'Who?' I heard him say as he soared past, purple scales shining in the light of the fires he'd set.

I informed him who I was, at volume, and with some asperity.

He returned to hover gracelessly near the window, and peered at me. 'I remember you,' he said.

'I should hope so! What will the next Mayor of Dapplehaven say when he hears you've been attacking the spire?'

Archibald brightened at that. 'He's here?'

'No, not just now, but he will be joining us later.' I hoped that last part wouldn't turn out to be a lie. 'He would be most disappointed, Archie. Why would you attack Melmidoc and Drystan's home?'

'I thought you were here to destroy it,' he said in an injured tone. 'Some people are coming to take it down. A Redclover told me. She said I should come here and burn anybody who gets near the spire.'

That must be what Mabyn had meant when she'd said she had "set something in motion". To be fair to her, she hadn't known at the time that Zareen and I would be here. 'She was right,' I told Archie. 'There are some people coming to ruin Melmidoc's home, but it isn't us. We're here to stop them.'

'Oh.'

'So no more fires, all right?'

Archibald tasted the air with his long, slithery tongue. Since no more gouts of fire were forthcoming, I took this gesture for assent.

The smoke was beginning to choke me and those licking flames were just a touch unnerving, so I devoted the next couple of minutes to summoning a nice smatter of rain. When I had water pouring suitably out of the cloudless sky, and the flames were winking out with dampened, hissing noises, I turned back to Zareen.

To my relief, she had stopped whatever it was she had been preparing to do. Her eyes were normal again, and her face was regaining some colour. I did not quite like the look of her satisfied smile, though.

'Zar, you didn't...?'

'I was about to stop!' she said. 'Promise! Only I'd already found Melmidoc by then.'

Slumbering in great comfort beneath an old favourite stone, said a voice, in deep, earthy tones that rumbled up from the starstones themselves. *And she hath had the temerity to disturb me.*

'But it *was* necessary,' said Zareen. 'Did you not say so, a moment ago?'

If my spire is aflame then perhaps it was, admitted Melmidoc.

'The fire's under control now,' I put in, but at the same time as I spoke there came a gasp from Archibald and he bellowed, *'Mel!'*

Silence, for a moment, and then the stones rumbled: *Is that Archibaldo?* He pronounced it *ark-i-bal-doe.*

'MEL!' screamed Archibaldo. There followed a great, crashing thud, and the graceful, delicate spire rocked upon its foundations. The dragon had thrown himself at the wall in his enthusiasm, and bounced off. More or less.

Hold, Archibaldo! shouted the stones of the spire. *Contain this unseemly jubilation! We are aged, and cannot withstand such an onslaught.*

'Sorry!' panted Archibaldo. 'But *Mel!* MEL!'

That is my name, or some little piece of it. It is good to see that you live, old friend.

'I do!' said Archie, and then remembered his purpose. 'Mel, some people are coming to destroy your house! We have to go!'

What? snapped Melmidoc. Archie proceeded to give a somewhat garbled account of the imminent danger to the spire, elucidated by my interpolations. I expected anger from Melmidoc and some kind of urgency, but he gave only a long, weary sigh. *I see.*

'We go!' crowed Archie. 'Back to the isle! It's been so *long,* I wonder if Drys is still there? And the others? Can we go now?'

We do not go to the isle, said Melmidoc, cutting off Archie's warbles of delight.

'But why not?' said Archie, crestfallen.

We do not go anywhere, Archibaldo. It is high time I departed this world.

I mentally reviewed the obstacles presently facing our stated mission. A Ministry rabid for the destruction of ancient and irreplaceable buildings; our Waymaster missing and incommunicado; Dappledok pups popping up left, right and centre; historic buildings wandering about through space and time, piloted by homicidal maniacs; and now a suicidal ghost.

It's never dull at the Society, I can tell you.

'Please reconsider,' I begged Melmidoc. 'Your home is valuable beyond measure, and we came here to save it.'

Not everything can be saved, nor should it be.

'And we would have speech with you,' I continued, and paused. Apparently Melmidoc's slightly antiquated articulation was rubbing off on me. 'There's so much you know, so much you've done! All those wonderful creatures, this spire, the — oh, and what is the isle? Please don't leave us just yet, not when we're just getting to know you.'

Flattery softens the hardest of hearts, it's sometimes said, and I've broadly found it to be true. Melmidoc wavered. I judged this from the long pause that followed, and a creaking among the stones of the spire that sounded, in some odd way, thoughtful.

My achievements, said Melmidoc at last. *Spurned and reviled by those that named themselves authorities! We retreated to the isle, but they could not let us have even that.*

'The isle?' I prompted again.

But Melmidoc did not answer. He lapsed into a brooding silence, leaving Zareen and I to exchange an uncertain glance. What more could we, or should we, do?

'I bet Drys is still there,' came Archibaldo's voice from the window. 'I miss him. Can we go and see him?'

I wonder if he is, said Melmidoc, in so low a whisper I almost failed to catch it.

Then the spire began to move. Not smoothly, like a car drifting into motion, but with a swaying, lumbering sensation — as though it had literally grown legs and walked away. I fell against the window and clutched it, white-knuckled, aghast at how close I had come to falling out.

A glance through the shattered panes — when had that happened? — revealed that we were not in Nautilus Cove anymore. A forest lay spread before us, predominantly composed of coniferous trees, with the glitter of still water somewhere ahead.

Another great, wrenching lurch of movement and the forest was replaced by the rugged slopes of a mountainside. Melmidoc was moving the spire after all, but not the way Jay did, from starting point to destination in one smooth(ish) hop. He bounced from place to place, darting about like a hyperactive bird, settling only briefly in each spot before dashing off to the next.

Interesting.

'Steady!' I yelled, as with another gigantic step of Melmidoc's I was almost turfed out of the window again.

This proved to be a mistake, for he stopped so abruptly that I was thrown the other way, and sent sprawling onto the stone-tiled floor. *Ah,* said Melmidoc. *Yes.*

And with those two laconic syllables, a violent wind blew up in the space of an indrawn breath, and sent me whirling out of the window into chilly fresh air. Something caught me halfway down; I felt a sensation like invisible fingers closing around my middle, and my precipitate fall slowed dramatically. I landed in mossy grass, quite gently, and Zareen joined me a moment later.

We both watched in crestfallen silence as the glorious spire gathered itself and jumped away, leaving us behind.

'Well,' I said after a while. 'We saved it.'

Zareen just grunted.

I scrutinised her. 'Are you all right?'

'Yes.'

'You sure?'

'Yes.'

I peered. The shadows had deepened under her eyes; she looked like she hadn't slept for a week.

Her eyes narrowed. 'Yes. I love you, but I did not confide in you so you could start your mother hen routine on me.'

I opened my mouth to object, but she forestalled me. 'Don't deny it! You cluck and fuss and it's sweet that you care, but I don't need it.'

Unsure what to say, I maintained an abashed silence.

This, perhaps, made Zareen just a touch guilty, for she relented and said: 'I'll be fine, I promise.'

I gave her a Miranda-style mini-salute, and turned my attention to the problem of where we had ended up.

We were no longer in Nautilus Cove, that was for certain. The pearly sea was gone, as was the frondy slopes that had led down to it. We had been plonked down in the middle of a wide expanse of clover-studded grass — indeed, in the grass versus clover wars the latter was winning by a mile. Nothing much beckoned upon the horizon, until I turned, and discovered the outlines of a town not too far distant. Dainty white clover blossoms carpeted the ground, but I detected a break in the otherwise ceaseless vegetation nearby, which proved to be a road. A handsome, well-kept one, too, very wide, and paved in clean white stones.

Zareen and I stepped onto it and began a brisk walk in the direction of the town. 'I think...' I mused as we walked.

'I mean, I wouldn't like to say that I'm sure, but I think I know where we are.'

'Really.' Zareen's voice dripped with scepticism.

'It's the clover,' I explained. I bent and plucked a leaf to show Zareen. 'They all have four leaves, or five.'

Her brows snapped down at that. 'Don't tell me we're in Ireland.'

'Oh, no! I know shamrocks and leprechauns are often grouped together but that's a circumstantial tie, there is no actual link. And anyway, the shamrock has three leaves, not four. We're actually in Wales. If I'm right, we're in the Glannyd Ceiriog Troll Enclave, and that town is Glannyd Pendry.'

'Lovely,' said Zareen. 'And where in all of Wales is that?'

I had to think about that for a moment. 'Um, the Ceiriog Valley, as I recall, is in northern Wales.'

'How far from home?'

I didn't have to think about that at all. 'Far.'

'Excellent.'

'Don't worry. I have a plan.'

I really did, and it wasn't even one of my crazy plans (as Jay would put it). It goes back to that sort of-date I had with the Baron the other week — the one where he'd whisked me off to Rhaditton for a pancake breakfast? I'd had little to do with the Troll Roads before, because they're not open to anyone who isn't, well, a troll. Or escorted by one with serious privileges. But now that I knew they were a) there, b) genuinely amazing, and c) not absolutely one-hundred-percent off-limits to non-trolls, I'd do my level best to make use of them more often.

Only in an emergency, though, which this rather was.

The town of Glannyd Pendry is one of those that drips money. I don't quite know how, for the Ceiriog Valley isn't exactly central and there is little real footfall up there. It's one of those that had a greater prominence in some past age and, unlike many others, managed to hold onto its prosperity. Anyway, we approached a town bristling with large, handsome, troll-sized buildings, most of them made out of the same clear white stones as the road we'd come in on. They were dazzling in terms of their architecture, all pediments and columns and huge, glittering windows. The air smelled of clover nectar, on the outskirts, but as we travelled deeper into the town that faded away in favour of one of my favourite aromas: that of good things to eat. I could have cheerfully stayed for a week.

Pity that we did not have that kind of time.

We attracted a little attention as we sauntered, with our best attempt at nonchalance, through the wide, well-kept streets, for there were many citizens abroad, but besides ourselves there were few humans. Always on the short side, I felt positively dwarfed in comparison to the good trolls of Glannyd Pendry, for not a one of them stands an inch less than six and a half feet, and plenty of them are rather taller. I felt like a child again: short, and lost in a confusing sea of perambulatory trees.

I had hoped to be able to find my way back to the coach-stop unaided, but being me this proved impossible. In my defence, it must've been at least five years since my last visit to the town. I stopped a couple of the more friendly-looking passers-by, and with their (slightly be-grudging) help Zar and I arrived at a positively enormous coaching inn within half an hour of entering the town.

Whereupon I called the good Baron.

'Alban,' I said as his voice came upon the line. 'I have a deal of interesting information to share, and quite the story to tell, but in exchange I'm in need of a little help.'

8

'YOU KNOW YOU DON'T have to bargain, Ves,' said Baron Alban in his lovely congenial way. 'I am, as ever, happy to help.'

I beamed into the phone. 'Well then, I'll give you all the details over a pancake or something, but here's the situation...'

Even the abbreviated version took me a couple of minutes to tell, time which Zareen spent roaming around inspecting the gathered coaches with some interest. They really were coaches, not the species of bus which is these days awarded that name: tall, bulky vehicles with huge wheels and big windows. The difference between these and the horse-drawn varieties of old was simply the lack of horse. There wasn't a beast of burden in sight, and none of the coaches had traces to attach a horse to. They didn't work that way.

Zareen was clearly intrigued.

'Do you have any idea where the spire went?' said the Baron as I finished my tale. He sounded rather urgent about it, too.

'No, except that Melmidoc mentioned an "isle" a couple of times so I wonder if that's where he was going. Before you ask, no, I don't know anything more about it. He said nothing else of use.'

'An isle,' mused the Baron. 'What does that book of yours say about it?'

'I haven't asked him yet. We've been busy with the business of getting out of here. But I was hoping to consult him on the coach-ride home.'

'Ah,' said the Baron, and I could almost see his eyes twinkling with amusement. 'I perceive we come to the favour.'

'If you could get us onto one of those coaches,' I said, 'we would be eternally grateful. Otherwise it'll take us all day to get home, and that's a monumental waste of time.'

'Give me a moment.' The Baron rang off.

I joined Zareen. 'Never seen these before?'

She shook her head. 'How do they move?'

'Magick.'

She rolled her eyes. 'I guessed that, but—'

My phone rang, and I grabbed it. 'Yes?'

'Someone'll be there to help you in a few minutes,' said the Baron.

'You're a hero. Thank you.'

'Don't forget about that pancake date. I won't.' He hung up.

I beamed upon Zareen and gave a contented sigh. 'It's *good* to have friends,' I told her.

'Especially important ones?'

'There are times when that's useful.'

'This being one of them. That I will grant you.'

A woman came towards us at that moment — seven feet tall if she was an inch — and looked Zareen and I over appraisingly. She wore a long dress of indeterminate period, a practical periwinkle-blue garment devoid of fuss or flounces, with the sleeves rolled up over her elbow. She said something in the lilting Welsh tongue.

'I'm afraid we aren't Welsh-speakers,' I apologised.

Her scowl deepened. 'I asked how did you two come to have Baron Alban at your beck and call?'

She did not seem pleased at the idea. 'I helped him with a couple of problems,' I offered.

Her brows went up. 'Oh? And what were they?'

Clearly his orders weren't quite enough to win us this woman's goodwill. 'Some of the Enclaves were endangered,' I said briefly. 'We were able to save most of them.'

Her face cleared. 'The Blight? That was you? Then, ladies, it shall be my pleasure to put a coach at your disposal.' To my mild embarrassment, she made us something of a bow. 'I have a cousin at Baile Monaidh,' she explained.

'It was our pleasure to help,' I said.

Our suddenly congenial hostess had us ensconced inside a comfortable coach within minutes, which was lucky because Zareen was beginning to look wan and peaky. Her admonishment about fussing and clucking in mind, I did not say anything about it, but I was privately glad that she'd have chance to sit down for a while. The seats were unusually plush, upholstered in something velvety and blue, and wide enough for Zareen to recline in an almost fully recumbent posture. She did so with studied casualness; I suspect it would've killed her to admit that she felt weak.

We thanked the coach mistress fervently and settled in for a long, but not too long, ride as the coach began to roll. We were set to be taken all the way back to Yorkshire, as near to the Scarlet Courtyard as the Troll Roads could take us.

Not quite as good as Waymastery, all told, but pretty close.

I opened up my shoulder bag and withdrew Gallimaufry. 'Right, Maufy,' I said, extracting my new book and Zareen's from his clutching embrace. 'What do you have to tell us?'

'Good afternoon, Miss Vesper,' said Mauf. 'Upon which topic am I requested to enlighten you?'

I passed the pamphlet on the Stranger Arts to Zareen, who took it with a notable lack of enthusiasm. 'Let's begin with the isle. You've got the Redclover brothers' journals, yes? Was there anything in there about an isle, or an island, or anything like that?'

Mauf lay inert and silent for a moment, thinking. Or consulting his records, or whatever it was he did. 'No,' he said at last.

'Damnit.'

'That is…' He paused. 'There was an entry towards the end of the journal which I had difficulty in deciphering, for large parts of it have been inked over. I am almost certain that one of the words in that particular section is "isle", but it is impossible to decipher the sentence as a whole. I am very sorry, Miss Vesper.'

'It isn't your fault,' I assured him, though I was inwardly cursing those guards back at Dapplehaven. They had taken the original copies of those books from us. I had thought nothing of it at the time, being supremely confident in Mauf's ability to absorb any text that came in his way. I had reckoned without the possibility that some of it might not have been legible.

'Still,' said Zareen sleepily. 'Interesting enough. Melmidoc wrote about it, then changed his mind and crossed it out. Why? Supposedly these were his personal journals.'

'I suppose nothing stays personal when you're a legend,' I said. 'And here is the proof of it. Hundreds of years later, and the likes of us are poking around trying to figure out what he was up to. He probably excited plenty of similar curiosity at the time.'

'Mm, and he did not want any of *those* busy-bodies finding out about this island.'

'So it's a secret island. Better and better. Mauf, did you get much else out of the Dapplehaven books that seemed to be of interest?'

Mauf thought again, and while he did that I sent a sneaky text to Valerie. Well, why not? We weren't technically working together just now, but that meant exactly nothing. She sent us books; I sent her info. Business as usual.

'Melmidoc was certainly a Waymaster,' Mauf began. 'And a very powerful one. Drystan, however, is something of a mystery. His particular arts are not explicitly discussed anywhere in the journals, though there are hints and references enough to suggest that he, too, possessed unusually potent powers.'

Zareen's eyes snapped open at that, and her gaze met mine. I could see she was thinking the same thing I was thinking. Drystan was a mighty sorcerer but the brothers had some motive to keep the nature of his powers a secret?

'Stranger Arts?' I said.

'Sounds like it,' said Zareen. 'And since this Waymastery business has been oddly bound up with the weird stuff all the way through, it figures.'

'Mm.' And an odd connection it was, too, for Waymastery and the Stranger Arts typically had little to do with one another — at least, these days. But I had to admit, the combination was proving to be a potent one. The two practices combined produced places like the Greyer Cottage and Millie Makepeace's house, not to mention the Starstone Spire itself. Who wouldn't want to run with that? Who could fail to be entranced by the possibilities?

Which put me in mind of something else. 'Mauf, you've said before that the journals don't specifically mention travelling through time. But is there anything to suggest that such an account might also be among those that were erased?'

'I cannot say, Miss Vesper. The passages in question have been thoroughly excised.'

'Whereabouts are they? The crossed-out parts.'

'Clustered largely towards the end, with a few exceptions scattered throughout the latter half of the book.'

'The last entries were in 1630?'

'That is correct.'

And Melmidoc Redclover had vanished in 1630, for the final time, never to be seen again — as far as history has recorded, at any rate. What had prompted him to disappear? Why had he never come back?

Well — that wasn't true. He had come back, because we had found him living (if his ghostly state could reasonably be termed such) in Nautilus Cove, still in his beloved home. So spire and Waymaster both had returned from wherever they'd gone to; but perhaps neither had ever returned to Dapplehaven.

Or had they? I remembered the spikes at the top of the hill, upon which the spire had once tended to rest. Jay and I had surmised that they were there to discourage the spire from settling there any longer; when had they been erected?

I shook my head, dissipating this string of thoughts. I had no answers as yet, and the spiralling questions were only confusing me. 'What about Millie Makepeace's diary?' I asked Mauf.

'Intriguing lady,' Mauf answered, with a touch of amusement. '*I am innocent of these disgraceful charges!*' he recited in a higher voice than his own, a woman's voice. '*To be sure, I attacked that foolish cook. Anyone would have done the same! She had put in far too much rind, and so bitter it was that I could not eat the pudding at all! It is not too much to expect of a cook, is it, that she should prepare a satisfactory orange-pudding? I threw the remainder, dish and all, at her foolish head, and she thoroughly deserved it! She screamed fit to bring the bricks tumbling around our ears, and made as though to come after me, but I was able to escape such vulgar treatment and retreated into the garden. Thus much is true. But I did not kill her! For though she is inept in the preparation of an orange-pudding, there is none to match her skill at bread-pudding, or carrot-pie. Was none, I should say, since the foolish woman is dead.'*

'Employer from hell,' murmured Zareen.

'The cook is said to have died from a wound to the head,' said Mauf. 'No further detail is given. Either, then, Miss Makepeace was assumed to have returned later to finish the deed with some other, suitably heavy object in hand as weapon; or perhaps the dish of orange-pudding did the job, and 'twas confectionery that killed the cook.'

I suppressed an inappropriate desire to giggle. The poor cook. 'I suppose it's just possible that someone else bashed in the woman's head?' I suggested.

'Quite possible,' allowed Mauf. 'But judging from the tone of her diaries I would conclude that Miss Make-peace was not of sound mind. She describes other violent episodes, and with a sublime lack of compunction.'

'Wandering off the point, Ves,' said Zareen. Her eyes had drifted shut again, but clearly she was still listening.

Right. Yes. It was a bit late to clear the name of Millie Makepeace, supposing she deserved it. She'd already been punished for the crime, and in a fashion that would normally prove awfully final. 'The diaries end with her execution?'

'The day before. You will be pleased to hear that she requested, and received, an orange-pudding as her final meal. One can only hope this one proved more satisfactory to her.'

'Mauf. Please stop making me laugh. It is inappropriate, given the subject matter.'

'Sorry, Miss Vesper,' said the book, without a trace of discernible remorse.

I wondered why Val had sent the book down, in that case. Perhaps just on spec. She must've dug it up at some speed, to send it down with Miranda.

I sent her another note. *Thanks for the books, by the way.*

Her reply came back at once. *What books? Working on the isle thing. Get back to you later.*

What books? I blinked at the screen in confusion. *The ones you sent with Mir?*

Zero books sent with Miranda, came the reply.

I showed this to Zareen, whose face registered the same puzzlement. 'I'm sure she said Val had given them to her.'

'That's what I thought, too.'

'Maybe we just assumed that.'

'Could be. Val is the usual source of books.' But I felt a vague sense of disquiet.

I toyed with the idea of contacting Miranda. I'm not close to her in the same way as I am with Val, or Zareen. In either of the latter cases I'd whizz off a text without a second thought, but to pester Miranda like that felt more like some kind of encroachment. It wasn't that Mir was unfriendly, but... she did not so much encourage hobnobbing.

I decided to try it anyway. I phrased a carefully-worded message idly enquiring where the books had come from, paired it with a bit of enthusiastic flattery as to their usefulness, and dispatched it. I was not surprised to find that no immediate reply came.

Something buzzed, but this time it wasn't me. Zareen rolled her eyes and fished her phone out of some obscure pocket. 'Tired,' she said laconically. 'Better be important.'

She listened, and as she did so her face clouded over. Then she became, suddenly, alert. 'What? Where is he? You haven't hurt him, have you?' She listened a moment more, then said: '*Fine,* I'm sorry, but how do you know all this?' After that, she was silent for so long, I could hardly bear it. Who did she mean by *he,* and who was she talking to? What had made her frown like that?

Finally, she said a curt, 'Right. Thank you,' and chucked her phone onto the coach seat. Her eyes were narrowed, and she still said nothing, nor looked at me at all.

'Zar,' I said at last, in what I hoped was a voice of cool composure but came out rather strained. 'Do tell.'

'George,' she said. 'Knows where Jay is, or so he claims. He knows about Millie Makepeace, somehow, too. He wants to exchange information.'

9

'Where's Jay?' I said quickly.

'He hasn't said. But he will, if we agree to share what we know.'

'Part of that pact you helpfully set up?' I subjected Zareen to my best slitty-eyed stare.

'Yes,' she said, unperturbed. 'And if he does know what's become of Jay, then it probably was helpful, wasn't it?'

I held up my hands in surrender, for Zareen's words emerged icily, and her face was set in bitter lines. 'What does he want in return?'

'Everything we know about the Redclovers and the spire. But, he says he's got more to share than just news of Jay. More about Millie, and others like her.'

'He didn't mention an isle?'

'Not so far. I wanted to ask, but if he hasn't heard about that yet I didn't want to give him ideas. And he probably hasn't, if he's short of information about Melmidoc and Drystan.'

'Maybe, but we don't know that this island belonged to the Redclovers, or that they had control of it. Could be something else entirely.'

'Could be. Ves, I know we've had this argument already but I really think joining forces with George would be to our mutual benefit. Right now we are groping around in the dark, trying to find stuff out for ourselves while also figuring out what *they* already know. Why not just cut the crap?'

I couldn't deny that she had a point. But. 'Zar, I hate to speak ill of your friend but he did try to kill us that one time.'

'He said he's sorry for trying to knock you off Addie.'

'Good of him.'

'He wasn't really trying to, you know. He's a deadly shot. If he'd wanted to kill you, he would have.'

'Then why shoot at us at all?' I remembered the day in question clearly: Jay had whisked us off to a new henge near Milton Keynes. We'd thought ourselves safe, but George Mercer and Katalin Pataki had followed. We had narrowly escaped upon the back of my beloved winged unicorn, while Mercer employed the most potent arts his

Sardonyx Wand had to offer to knock us to the ground again. We'd been carrying Bill at the time, that was the crux of it: the very first book like Mauf, intelligent and communicative and packed with a dizzying amount of information. Everybody wanted him.

'Ask him sometime,' Zareen suggested.

'Like when?'

'Like at the Ashdown Castle Ball, which is tomorrow.'

So it was. I had forgotten about it. 'I was really hoping to have Jay back by tomorrow.'

'You might do. Who knows?'

I tried calling Jay again, with the same results as ever. Nothing. Failure to connect, and he had not read my messages.

I stared at the evidence of this in silence for a while. 'Zar, how far do you have to go to get zero phone or internet service?'

'Honestly? Not that far.'

I'd begun to wonder whether Millie had carted Jay off to, say, 1768, but Zar was right. Chuck him on a suitably remote mountaintop and the effect would likely be much the same.

But I hated not knowing. Above all things that I *hate*, it's ignorance.

'How could George know where Jay is?' I asked.

'He didn't precisely say. He implied, though, that John Wester and Millie Makepeace aren't the only examples of their peculiar capabilities and that Ancestria Magicka's got a tame one.'

Hardly surprising, really. I'd guessed since the Greyer Cottage that they were after a pet Waymaster, preferably undead, and with the kinds of resources they had, of course they'd achieved it. In record time. While we were still flailing around, bumping into Millie Makepeace by accident.

Still, George wanted something from us. That meant we were ahead of them somewhere.

'Here's my counter-offer,' I said crisply to Zareen. 'I don't just want to know where Jay is. I want him to take us there. If he's got a tame walkabout house then that should be easy for him.'

Zareen gave me her weird, twisted smile. 'Thought you'd say that.' There followed a brief phone conversation in which she relayed this to Mercer, and soon rang off. 'Deal,' she told me. 'If Jay's not back by tomorrow, he'll take us to him.'

I wondered whether that hadn't been just a bit too easy, but I said nothing. Zar might be caught in a difficult position just now, but I trusted her. She might be chummier with Ancestria Magicka than I liked, but she would never betray the Society. Or me.

I hung onto that certainty with both hands.

WE REACHED THE SCARLET Courtyard just in time for dinner, which pleased my stomach greatly for (as I had begun to realise about halfway through the coach journey) we had managed to skip lunch.

Alas, food was not to be mine for a little while yet, because it turned out to be one of those occasions where everything happens at once.

Mrs. Amberstone met us as we trooped wearily through the hallway. She smelled enticingly of something that was probably pie. 'Visitor for you, girls,' she said. 'Chap from the Society.'

Intriguing. 'Thanks, Mrs. A. Whereabouts is he?'

'Somewhere about the gardens. Seems restless.'

That did not bode well, but I tried not to worry about it as I traipsed upstairs with Zareen. I wanted a quick change of clothes and a drink of water before I dealt with the next problem.

Halfway up the stairs to our rooms, though, my pocket buzzed.

Got them from Val, Miranda had sent. *Anything good in there?*

I stopped dead, frozen with astonishment. I read it a couple of times, just to be sure, before I showed it to Zareen.

She said nothing. There was nothing to say.

I hauled the two books out of my shoulder-bag again and snapped a quick shot for Val.

It didn't take long for her to reply. *Where did you get those, and can I have them?*

From Mir, I wrote back. *Says she got them from you?*

Those did not come from this library, Val replied.

I sat slowly down upon the steps and put my face in my hands, because as bad news went, this bordered upon awful. I was not quite so appalled as I would have been had it been Valerie or Zareen, or Rob, or Jay. But it was bad enough.

How far back did it go?

'Why would Miranda lie about that?' said Zareen. She'd joined me on the step, less because she was shocked, I suspected, than because she was exhausted.

'I can only think of one reason. If those books didn't come from our library and Mir's concealing the source, then they came from someplace she should not have access to.'

Zareen just nodded, her head drooping wearily.

'Shit,' I muttered, and hauled myself to my feet again. The question of why Miranda had gone out of her way to put those books into our hands, even at the risk of discovery, could wait. First I had to find out who had come from the Society.

It was Rob, of course. We found him pacing about under the walnut trees at the back of Mrs. Amberstone's garden, brow uncharacteristically clouded. He wore his customary dark shirt and trousers, and a dapper fedora over his dark curls. This last he took off, and rubbed a hand over his hair. The gesture looked unutterably weary.

'Bad news, I'm afraid,' he said as we approached. 'I didn't want to tell you over the phone.'

'It's Miranda, isn't it?' I said.

'How did you know that?' There was a tilt to his head and a wary quality to his voice that I did not like. Was this how it would be from now on? Would we all suspect each other?

'Miranda's been at somebody else's library, and I suspect it's Ancestria Magicka's.' I showed Rob the few messages she and I had exchanged, and the books themselves.

Rob just looked at them, and gave a soft sigh. 'That's it, then.' He shook his head, and gave the books back to me. 'Might as well get some use out of those before we have to give them back.'

I stashed them again.

'How did *you* find out?' said Zareen.

'I told you there's been a rash of Dappledok puppies turning up? Miranda kept going out to collect them, but wherever she was taking them, it wasn't Home. That became clear about an hour ago. Then we realised she hadn't come back at all from the last pickup, had left no word for anybody, and — and she's taken several of the rarest beasts from the East Wing. At least, nobody knows where they are, so it's the most likely explanation.'

It physically hurt to hear this. Miranda was a fixture at the Society, had been for almost as long as I'd been employed there. How could she? What was she *thinking*?

I saw some of the same questions written over Rob's face. 'Has anyone spoken to her?' I asked.

He shook his head. 'She hasn't been answering her phone, or messages.'

'She answered me,' I said, already typing. *Where are you*? That's all I put.

Perhaps unsurprisingly, this message she did not answer.

'Was it Mir, then, who told Ancestria Magicka about Bill?' I said, trying to maintain my composure. 'And put the tracker spell into the book?'

Rob shrugged. 'Hard to say until someone gets hold of her, but it looks likely.'

'But why?' I could think of nothing else to say.

'She's always been so passionate about those beasts,' said Rob, and as devastated as he was himself he was still kind enough to lay a comforting hand on my shoulder. 'The Society has always had to follow Ministry policy there. Imagine how tempting it must have been to her, when Ancestria Magicka appeared. Money to do anything and everything necessary for her creatures, and the will to defy the Ministry if they deemed it important enough. Imagine what they must have promised her. And then you showed up with a Dappledok pup...'

I was gripped by a sudden fear. 'Rob. My pup — or not *my* pup, but, you know — did Miranda take her as well?'

Rob nodded. 'I'm sorry, Ves. There are no pups left at Home.'

'*Damnit,* Miranda.' I took a breath, and ruthlessly pulled myself together. 'When we saw her this morning, she had a couple of unfamiliar kennel aides with her. I assumed they must be new recruits.'

'As far as I know, not. We haven't had any newcomers in the Beasts division lately.'

'So they were probably from Ancestria Magicka.'

Rob nodded.

I realised Zareen was no longer with us. Looking around, I saw her several feet away, her phone to her ear. She had the tense, listening posture of a person hearing unwelcome news.

'George Mercer,' I said. 'Bet that's who she's talking to. If Miranda's been working for them these past weeks, he probably knew.'

'And didn't tell her?' Rob winced in sympathy.

'He wouldn't, would he? But I think Zar believes he's honest with her.' Privately, I think she needed to believe that. Mercer was more important a figure in her world than he at all deserved to be, at least in my opinion.

'Something doesn't add up, though,' I said, frowning. 'Why did Mir get us those books?'

Rob thought that over. 'I've known Miranda many years,' he said after a while. 'Whatever misdeeds she may have lately committed, I don't believe she's ruthless by na-ture, nor would betrayal have come easily to her. If she did put the tracker spell in your book, she probably thought her new allies would just steal it. She could never have meant for you or Jay to end up in harm's way.'

'So you think this is guilt?' I slapped a hand against my shoulder-bag, where the purloined books lay.

Rob grimaced. 'Something like that. More a desire to make amends, perhaps. And... just because she's been helping Ancestria Magicka, doesn't mean she's become entirely disloyal to the Society.'

'How good of her to help us,' I muttered.

Rob gave me a sad smile, and I felt a bit guilty. But, then, Rob had heard this news a little sooner, and he'd had time to regain his composure. I hadn't, yet, but I would get there.

'Wait,' I said, another thought breezing cheerily into my over-burdened head. 'What about Lord Garrogin? He interviewed Mir, like the rest of us. Why didn't he know?'

'Those questions are being asked.'

Much good it would do us. Garrogin would deny all knowledge, and it might be the truth or it might not be.

I called the Baron.

It hurt so much, to have to tell him of Miranda's treachery. He listened in silence, however, and when I raised Lord Garrogin's name he became unusually grim.

'Miranda's not a sorceress or a witch or — or anything, Alban,' I finished. 'She doesn't have a great deal of magick of her own. What she does have is a few charms and cantrips that keep her beasts calm and happy; a bit of healing magick; that kind of thing. Nothing, in short, that could help her to deceive a Truthseeker.'

'Right,' said the Baron, his voice wintry-cold. 'Then he's a turncoat, too.'

'Looks like it.'

Baron Alban sighed. 'Thanks, Ves. I'll tell Their Majesties.'

Zareen came back, her face white and set. 'We're going to that party,' she informed me.

'Oh?'

'And we may or may not be burning down the castle on our way out.'

10

I SENT A FEW messages to Miranda after that, mostly variations on the general theme of *why?*

To my regret, but not to my surprise, she did not answer any of them.

By the next morning, it was official: Miranda had gone. Rob brought us a copy of the Society's internal memo on the subject.

I winced upon reading it. Milady was most seriously displeased.

Miranda Evans is no longer a member of this Society. The circumstances of her departure are not for public dissemination. Let it be known, however, that any and all communication with Ms. Evans is strongly discouraged.

There was more, but not much. I pictured the icy fury with which Milady had penned the missive (or dictated it, she being incorporeal and all) and shuddered.

It did raise an interesting question, though. Had Miranda corrupted anybody else, prior to her departure? I could only assume that was the fear lurking behind Milady's prohibition on communication. We none of us wished to lose any more people to Ancestria Magicka.

I'd had to field a string of messages from Indira, too. She had discovered Jay's absence by way of several failed and unanswered phone calls and was cheerfully freaking out about him. Since I was in much the same state, albeit more secretly, there was not much I could do to reassure her. I could not even say for sure that George Mercer's offer was still open, not after he and Zareen had so obviously fallen out over Miranda.

Difficult morning. I treated my nerves to an extra helping of chocolate from Milady's wonderful pot, recruited my strength with some of Mrs. Amberstone's best pancakes, and boosted my confidence with a change of hair colour. Maybe it sounds frivolous, but try it before you judge me.

I stepped out a little later, tossing my parti-coloured hair (cream at the top and daffodil-yellow at the bottom, with a smooth ombre fade in between). I was beginning to lose my patience with this particular mess, and it was high time we sorted it out.

I found Zareen in much the same frame of mind. A solid ten hours of sleep had restored her colour somewhat, and she looked much nearer her old self when she opened her door. 'Plan?' she said.

'Find Jay.' I ticked off *point one* on my fingers. 'Find out what that isle of Melmidoc's is about. Figure out what the bloody hell has got into Miranda and fix it. Discover the source of the Dappledok pups and fix that, too. And find out once and for all where in space or time those houses are going to when they vanish.' I ticked them all off on my fingers, using rather more fingers in the process than I was hoping.

'That's a wish list,' said Zareen. 'What's the *plan?*'

'No bloody clue.'

'Right, then. Situation normal.' Zareen grabbed her jacket, stuffed her feet into her boots and fell in beside me as I made for the stairs.

'The party's at seven,' Zareen said, checking the time. 'We've got ten hours until then. Pick a place to start?'

'Baron Alban.'

'Needing a little eye candy?'

'Always, but that's not it this time. Val's drawn a blank on Melmidoc's isle as far as our library goes, and Mauf has nothing for us either. We need another resource, and

I can't think of a better one than the library at the Troll Courts. Can you?'

'I can punch George in the face until he consents to check their records for us.'

'Think that'll work?'

'No. And anyway, I'd have to tell him all about the isle first, and we sort of agreed not to do that.'

'Right. Plan forming. Part one in progress.' I composed another message to Miranda and sent it before I could change my mind.

It said: *Rage aside, Mir, those books prove you want to help us. So help. Find out anything you can about a secret isle, probably 1600s, linked to names like Melmidoc Redclover. Please. Thanks xx*

We hadn't given Miranda the full low-down about the spire before, probably because it had not seemed relevant. We'd just told her about the part we knew would interest her: Dramary's Bestiary. I wondered, though. Had she heard the rest from someone else? Word tended to travel at Home. If she had, she would have taken that information to Ancestria Magicka — which meant that George Mercer must be lying about their ignorance. If so, what was his game?

I showed my message to Zareen, who grunted, a sound halfway between approval and irritation.

'I know, I know.'

'I hate this.'

'Me too. Right. Part two in progress.' I called the Baron. 'Alban,' I said crisply the moment he answered. 'It's Ves. May I speak frankly?'

'Please.'

'This shit is driving us crazy and we would like to resolve it. We propose a joining of forces.'

'Oh? Among whom, exactly?'

'The Thrilling Three, even if we are presently down to the Testy Two, and the Troll Court.'

'As represented by me?'

'Yes.'

I waited. I knew the Baron would understand my meaning. I wasn't just asking for his personal assistance; I was requesting the official aid of Their Majesties' Court itself.

'I'll see what I can do,' he said.

The Baron arrived in person about an hour later.

Zareen and I spent the intervening time scouring Miranda's books for what Nancy Drew might have called "leads" (unsuccessfully). About all I could determine from Millie Makepeace's diaries was that she was batshit crazy, and largely unaware of her Waymaster abilities. Apparently magickal education for young women of breeding was on the underwhelming side, back in the day. I wondered who had introduced her to her powers (after death...?), and how they had known she'd had any. I shied away from the idea that someone from her own family had been re-sponsible for her after-death fate, but one or two references to her father made me wonder a bit. Had he been a prac-titioner of the Weird Stuff? Perhaps.

Zareen read through her pamphlet with an irritable frown, and finally snapped it closed with, I thought, un-necessary violence. The booklet was old, and delicate. I gently took it from her. 'No use?'

'Tells me nothing new.'

Judging from her glowering dissatisfaction, it had re-minded her of a number of things she did not like to think about.

I checked the title. *Dark Deeds and Strange Wayes: The Wyrde Path.* No author was listed.

'It's all new to me,' I said. 'Mind if I read?'

Zareen had signalled her lack of objection with a shrug, and had then proceeded to stretch out in the grass (we were out in Mrs. Amberstone's garden again, under the walnut trees). Whether she was sleeping or brooding I could not tell.

I skimmed through the pamphlet, keeping an absent eye on my phone in case of word from the Baron or Miranda — or Mabyn Redclover, at the Hidden Ministry. I'd in-formed her of the fate of the spire, and had capitalised on her satisfaction by pleading for help. I knew Val would be doing her utmost to come up with something, too; with that many people at work on the matter of the mysterious isle, I had hopes of hearing something useful soon.

But the pamphlet.

'Chilling read,' I said when I'd finished it.

That was an understatement. It proved to be the work of an early serial killer. The author — who was so cagey about his or her identity that I could not even determine their gender — had discovered at a horrifyingly young age that the "art" of killing (their words, not mine) had a pleasurably amplifying effect upon their "wyrde wayes" (also their words). The obliging author had conducted a number of grisly murders over a period of years (all described in detail) and recorded the effects of these despicable deeds upon their unsavoury magicks. All very positive, I was to believe; after several such murders, the author was understood to be in possession of virtually unheard-of power in fields such as necromancy, and could *oblige any Ghoste or Spirite to do my Bydding,* as well as *making Puppets of the Deade,* and, perhaps most interestingly, *restorynge Life that has been Loste.*

Did they mean converting the *dead* into the *undead,* or a revival from death back into a state of genuine life? If the latter, that was... remarkable. I experienced a vision of this unknown necromancer four hundred years ago, killing the same victim over and over again in the name of experimentation, and shuddered. Thank goodness I had not been burdened with the Stranger Arts. I wouldn't have lasted five minutes at the School of Weird.

I was not absolutely convinced by the author's claims. The text displayed clear signs of narcissism and megalomania, in my humble opinion, and surely the links between murder and "wyrde" powers couldn't be that simple or powerful or we'd have seen a total ban on all such arts many years ago.

But Zareen accepted it, and she ought to know.

I handed the pamphlet back to her.

Message from Miranda. *Tread carefully, Ves.*

'Is that it?' I said in disgust, quoting it to Zareen. 'What the bloody hell is that supposed to mean?'

'Means she knows something but cannot or will not say, other than to imply that it is dangerous.'

I sighed. 'And that means Ancestria Magicka knows something, which means maybe it's time to start punching George in the face.'

Zareen complied, metaphorically speaking.

And then came the Baron, strolling over Mrs. Amberstone's neatly-trimmed lawn like he had all the time in the world. I suppose with those long legs, he could stroll all he liked and still make faster progress than I would at a brisk trot. He'd dressed down: he wore a pair of crisp, dark blue trousers and a loose white shirt, open at the neck. Polished shoes, no hat, his bronze-blonde hair artfully disordered.

If anything, the effect was more devastating than all the impeccable, elaborate style of his previous ensembles. He smiled at me as he approached, his green eyes bright with apparent pleasure at seeing me, and something odd happened in my stomach.

'Morning,' I said lightly.

Baron Alban made us a polite, courtly bow amid exquisitely courteous greetings. I did not imagine it: his smile definitely lingered on me. 'Morning, ladies. What's the news?'

'Not much.' I showed him Miranda's note, upon which he made no comment save for a raised eyebrow.

'I'd hoped you were bringing the cavalry,' I said, noticing all the empty space around him that was not filled with other knowledgeable and useful members of Their Majesties' Court.

'What, one wickedly handsome troll isn't enough for you?'

'Well, since you mention it...'

He grinned. 'I'm afraid it's just me, but I do bring help.'

I sat up. 'Oh?'

'I don't know if you realise it, but you and Jay are popular at Court at the moment — what with uncovering the blight at the lost enclaves, hacking your way into Farringale and coming out alive, and now tackling this spire business.'

'Their Majesties aren't opposed to investigating there?'

'No. It wouldn't be the first time they've disagreed with the Ministry. But Ancestria Magicka has them worried, and angry. Lord Garrogin was a friend.'

'Was?'

'Mm.' The Baron's mouth set in a grim line. 'He isn't anymore. His invitation to the Court has been revoked.'

'So, the isle?' I prompted.

'I drew a blank at the library. Nothing there. I can say this with certainty because Her Majesty interviewed our Chief Archivist on the subject personally. I never saw a man more terrified. I don't think he could have lied to save his life.

'But, the library is not our only resource. The Court is a court in two senses of the word: it's the home of Their Majesties, and it's also a place of justice. Has been ever since the fall of Farringale. A lot of cases have been heard there, and a lot of complaints lodged.'

I discreetly checked the time. Not discreetly enough, for the Baron saw me and smiled a wry smile. 'All right, the short version: I consulted the Scribe of the Court of Justice. One of his duties is to maintain the court's records, including recopying the oldest and most faded documents at need. And those date from the early sixteen hundreds through into the eighteen hundreds.

'Late last year he copied and refreshed an account of a complaint brought by one Talbot Makepeace, of Suffolk, who claimed that his house and his daughter had been stolen from him. The complaint was dismissed because his daughter was known to have been recently executed, and he could give no proper explanation as to how his house had been filched. He claimed it had walked away, and his dead daughter with it. I believe the poor man was written off as mad. He was noted to have shrieked something about *that accursed isle* as he was dragged from the Court.'

'Ah!' I crowed. 'A link between Millie and the isle!'

'Indeed.' The Baron paused to smile at me. 'Another, older complaint referred to an unnamed isle in a similar way. This one was dated to somewhere in the sixteen thirties, so the Scribe estimated, and it was a much more serious case. An attempt was made to prosecute one Melmidoc Redclover and his brother Drystan for the creation of a secret magickal society, one unauthorised by any power in existence. Now, they were not actually obliged to have permission in order to set up their own establishment; there was no such stringent system of laws then, as there are now. But if you wished to create a new magickal nation, with its own legalities and rules and its own, independent authority, it was considered polite to have the support of your peers. To act without it was to make a lot of people nervous, for what might you be planning to do? Melmidoc and Drystan skipped that part. The account, unfortunately, is not that useful, because the Redclover brothers could not be got hold of for comment. They'd disappeared, and so had the isle.'

11

I SAT UP VERY straight, electrified. 'The *isle* disappeared! An entire island! Impossible!'

'Apparently not,' said Alban.

'But then, its location was known initially?'

'Mm. It was said to lie about three and a half miles off the Yorkshire coast, about due east from the town of Scarborough.'

'But had it always been there? I've never heard of an island in those parts.'

'There certainly hasn't been for the past four hundred years. And there is no reason to imagine that it was a large island.'

'Even so.' My mind was awhirl at the prospect, but so was my scepticism. 'I know that Waymasters used to be a lot more powerful, and clearly they could — and *can*

— move buildings around. But so far, they're small ones. Cottages and modest farmhouses.'

'And the spire,' put in Zareen.

'Right, but even that isn't so huge a place. An entire island, though? A spit of land? I'm not sure I believe it.'

'Islands have been known to move about before,' said the Baron. 'Come loose and float away.'

'Fixed or not, it's still a big land mass. If it was habitable, it must have been at least a few miles square. How many Waymasters working together would it take to move all that? Surely it cannot be done.'

'And yet,' said the Baron. 'As far as the official enquiry records, it was gone.'

'They couldn't prove that it was gone,' I pointed out. 'All they meant was, they couldn't find it. Perhaps it was not gone, but hidden.'

The Baron inclined his head, ceding the point.

Maybe I shouldn't be so resistant to the idea that an island had physically moved. A few weeks ago, the idea that a two-room cottage could waltz off had seemed impossible.

'So the island existed,' I mused. 'And while we are not certain that the isle mentioned by Talbot Makepeace was the same one, it seems likely. Everything fits. So it was probably still there — or still *somewhere* — over a century and a half later, and somebody lured Millie there. Perhaps the same somebody who had awoken her Waymaster abilities in the first place, and bound her into the farmhouse.'

'But is the isle still there now?' said Zareen.

Melmidoc had rushed off to answer that same question. Had he succeeded in finding his lost isle? Or was it gone, sunk beneath the waves long ago?

If it was still there, was Millie still in the habit of frequenting the place?

Was that where she had taken Jay?

If it was, and the Baron's theory was correct, then the island could be anywhere. It didn't even have to be in British waters anymore. It could be lurking off the coast of New Zealand, or somewhere in the middle of the Indian Ocean.

Under the circumstances, I preferred my theory.

'I'm going to see George,' Zareen suddenly announced.

'What—' I began, but she was already striding away in the direction of the Scarlet Courtyard.

'Meet you at the party,' she called back.

'Right,' I said, taken aback.

The Baron raised an eyebrow.

I could only shrug. 'I do not know what's going on with them.'

'By the looks of it, I'd say a lot.'

'Zar knows what she's doing.'

'She does have the look of a formidable woman.' The Baron was twinkling at me again, damn him, which was as much as to say that I didn't.

Probably a fair observation, what with my daffodil hair. I straightened my spine a bit more, and rose with dignity to my feet. 'I have an alternative theory,' I told him.

'To my wild reports of wandering isles?'

'Yes. I need to see Val. Are you game for a sneak-in?'

'Sneaking into Home? Has it come to that? I thought you left on decent terms.' Did I imagine the slight emphasis he'd put on the word *left*? As though he was making air quotes in his mind while he said it.

'If you call defying Milady's orders about the spire decent behaviour, then yes, we left on excellent terms.'

That was definitely a smile lurking about his lips. 'As you say,' he said mildly.

I gave a sigh. 'It was Garrogin, wasn't it?'

'He did seem to think that you and Jay made a perfect picture of loyalty. The way he told it, well. I wish my staff were half as loyal.'

'Curse him.'

'Their Majesties have already done so.'

The twin curse of a pair of powerful troll royals ought to be a bit more effective than mine, so I let Lord Garrogin be.

TRUTH TO TELL, I was a bit uneasy about going back Home again so soon. I knew Milady would not mind in principle, but in practice? Our masquerade had already proved to be paper-thin. It was stupid to jeopardise it further by sauntering back Home just as though we still belonged there. It would have to be subterfuge.

Which is a tall order, because our House's security measures are deservedly legendary. Why do you think Ancestria Magicka went to so much trouble to get their claws into Miranda? It isn't like they could just send over a spy. They either had to get someone of their own recruited by Milady, or convert an existing Society employee; there were no other options. If Milady had revoked my access to Home, then there was no way I was getting in. Or the Baron either.

So it was with some trepidation — and some bitter feelings — that I approached the environs of our beloved House late that morning, riding as passenger in the Baron's beautiful sleek car. We parked just outside the entrance, and the fact that I could still see the handsome double gates reassured me a little. First layer of security: it is tricky to break into a place you cannot find.

I had the sense not to waltz in at the front gate; instead, we circled around to a side-door into the grounds, and slipped through. Nothing was barred, and nobody tried to stop us. The walk from there into the House itself was a short one, just down a narrow passageway lined with hedgerows, across the narrowest part of the shrubbery, and then in at the door.

Hopefully.

Beloved House. I had been banished from it for only a handful of days, and yet I experienced a piercing sense of loss as I walked up to the door and gazed wistfully up at its ancient walls. Not just Home, but *my* home, and for the past decade. Place of work, place of abode, place of everything. A small part of me harboured the fear that, one way or another, I might never be able to come properly Home again.

But that was foolish. This was just an assignment, like any other. Once we had established the truth (or lack thereof) about the spire, the island and the whole prospect of time travel, we would be able to return.

'Morning, House,' I said with a bright smile, and knocked lightly upon the heavy oak door. 'Is it all right if we go in to see Val?'

The door was unlatching even as I spoke, its bolts rattling as they drew back. Before I'd even got as far as uttering Val's name, the door swung wide open with a cheerful creak. Was I being fanciful in interpreting it as a welcoming sound?

I went inside, laying a hand briefly upon the white-plastered wall as I went past. 'I miss you too,' I told the dear old place.

Baron Alban followed me into the passage. We were in what had once been the servants' wing of the house; the old scullery was to our left, and on the right were the pantries. Some of those were still used to store food. 'Do you and the House always chat like that?' asked the Baron.

'Yes, always.' I spoke absently, for it occurred to me that my plan had been limited. All right, we were inside: but how were we to make it as far as the library without passing at least a few people?

I trod softly to the end of the passage and peeked around the corner. No one in sight, yet, but a couple of passages and a few corners down that way, we'd enter the library complex, and it was a popular spot. There was no way we could sneak—

'Ves!' said Val.

I whirled.

She was right behind me, ensconced as usual in her majestic green velvet chair. She did not look so perfectly turned out as usual; her upswept dark hair was tumbling down a bit at the back, and her clothes had the rumpled look that suggested "freshly pressed" was an increasingly distant memory. 'Val?' I blurted. 'I was just—'

'Coming to find me. I know, House brought me. Bloody hell, Ves, where have you been?'

'We've been—'

'I mean, I know the official story but I've never heard so much crap in my life. As if you *or* Zareen would ditch us like that! Or Jay either!'

'I know, but it was necessary to—'

'*I've missed you.*' They might have been pleasant words but Val spat them out like they were the gravest insults, her eyes flashing fire.

'Val.' I held up my hands in a gesture of surrender. 'I thought Milady would have told you everything, I—' It occurred to me that we were not exactly in a secure location, so I shut up. 'Can we get somewhere quiet?'

Only then did Val notice the Baron, who had been loitering at a polite distance from us both. He sauntered up with a show of non-threatening casualness, and graced her with one of his courtlier bows.

Val's eyes went very wide. I tried to remember whether she had ever met the Baron in person before, and concluded that she probably had not.

He did tend to have an impact.

'This is Baron Alban, from the Court,' I said, to cover her silence.

Val held out a hand. 'It is a pleasure to meet any representative of Their Majesties of Mandridore, but do you mind if I ask what you're doing here?'

The Baron shook Val's hand with a smile. 'Helping Ves, actually.'

Val gave me a roguish look that said *well-I-never*, but her voice was steely again when she spoke. 'If you steal Ves away to Mandridore, Baron, I shall never forgive you.'

'Understood.'

'In fact, the entire Society will swarm Their Majesties' gates in order to fetch her back.'

Alban saluted gravely.

I was touched.

'Right,' Val said, more crisply. 'House, dear. Somewhere private for the three of us?'

A door opened silently in the wall to Val's left. A door that had not been there a moment before.

Val's wing-back chair floated serenely through it, and the Baron and I followed.

12

On the other side of the door was House's favourite room. I had been there just once before, in search of the third key to Farringale. In character it is a pretty sitting-room, a perfectly preserved specimen of mid-to-late seventeenth century style, with elegant floral wallpaper, wrought-silver candlesticks (never tarnished) and a tall grandfather clock. House keeps it well hidden.

Val sailed her chair over to a wall and stopped, promptly producing a laptop from somewhere. She started it up and began typing furiously.

I took one of the tall, pale-upholstered chairs, and spent a moment collecting my thoughts.

'What are we working with?' said Val. She'd stopped typing and was waiting expectantly.

'Lost islands,' I said.

'You mean like Atlantis?'

'A bit more real.'

'Atlantis isn't real?'

'It... is it?' I stared.

Val grinned. 'Might be.'

'You did say *is*, not *was*?'

With a flick of her fingers, Valerie waved this away. 'Another time. So like Atlantis or more like Ferdinandea?'

'That's the one that keeps vanishing and popping up again? No. No volcanic activity involved, as far as we know. It's more like Bermeja.' (I had done some research already).

'Gulf of Mexico,' said Val promptly. 'Marked on a few ancient maps but nobody can find it today?'

'Exactly. Or any sign that it ever existed at all.'

'Okay. But you're certain this island of yours did exist.'

I told her everything we'd heard so far, every miserably insufficient clue we had mustered, and spoken all together it did not sound like much. But Val listened with close attention, and as I'd hoped, the question fired her interest.

She began typing again.

'Could be vanished,' she murmured, half to herself. 'Islands vanish all the time, but they're usually discernible lying right there on the sea bed, and you say this one was never on any maps?'

'That's one of the questions I had for you. Can you find a map with an island marked off the Scarborough coast? Pre-sixteen-hundred, it would be.'

'Working on that. Really though, Ves, how could anybody hide an entire island? Especially so close to shore.'

'Well.' I sneaked a look at the Baron. 'Er. You know when you're working on a valuable book, and you want to take a bathroom break, but you don't want to have to put the book away only to haul it out again ten minutes later?'

Val stopped typing. Her face said: *You know about that?*

I gave her an apologetic look, and said no more. I'd seen her pull a sneaky trick with just such a book, once. It was incredibly rare, one of the few copies of *Agadora's Miscellany* still extant. The library had been empty other than the two of us, and I was at the other end of it, apparently absorbed in a book. Val had left the room — leaving the *Miscellany* on the table before her.

I thought she had forgotten to put it away, or perhaps trusted to me to guard it. But when I'd looked at the table, there was no book there. I went over to investigate, and I still couldn't find it, couldn't see it, couldn't feel it.

When Val came back, there it was again, in the same spot as before, as though it had never moved at all. Which, in all probability, it hadn't.

'So, that trick,' I continued. 'How big an, er, object could you hide like that?'

Val stared, wide-eyed, at nothing. 'No idea, Ves. I've never tried it on anything bigger than—' She broke off, shooting a faintly guilty look at the Baron. He, of course, just twinkled. 'I would not like to attempt it upon a significant land mass,' she finished.

'All right, we can hold that idea in reserve. What about the Baron's idea? Could it be moved around?'

Alban coughed politely. 'I did not actually intend to propose the notion as my own idea. It is merely a possibility that has surfaced.'

I inclined my head in his general direction. 'I'm going to keep calling it your idea anyway, because it's simpler than "the other idea that the Baron happened to raise but that does not necessarily reflect his private thoughts on the matter."'

He grinned. 'Fair enough.'

'Waiving for a moment the question of whether or not it's possible,' I continued, 'it is a plausible explanation. If I were Melmidoc Redclover, and Their Gracious Majesties were trying to prosecute me for breaking a million rules, I'd want to whisk my hideout somewhere far away too. But where would they go? It would have to be somewhere isolated enough that no one would stumble over it — and it seems nobody has, in all these years. But somewhere habitable, too. Survivable climate, source of food, and so on. Where in the world might that put them?'

This is where I wanted Val's help, aside from the matter of her book-hiding trick. She doesn't have a search engine so much as a search labyrinth, and as I talked her fingers moved ceaselessly over the keys of her laptop. She was feeding it endless lists of search terms, and as she worked her search-maze was scouring a host of databases for every nugget of relevant information (several of them seriously off-limits to most of us), cross-referencing everything with everything else, and hopefully pulling out something useful.

It occurred to me that the Baron had been quiet, for all his talk of helping. When I looked his way, I found that he was looking at me. I wish I could say it was an admiring look, but it was more of a thoughtful gaze, with a hint of something troubled in it.

I made a questioning face, but he only smiled and looked away.

'I am happy to tell you that there are exactly zero places on the planet that match those criteria,' said Valerie after a while.

'Zero!'

'It's the twenty-first century, Ves. We've had satellites for a while now. Nobody's hiding any mystery islands anymore.'

I felt an impulse to chew upon a fingernail, which I suppressed. It is a habit I broke years ago, but it still surfaces occasionally in times of stress. 'Then it is either hidden after all, or... there's the third possibility.'

'That being?'

'*You* know. We cannot find the isle because it's popped off to 1598. And so have Millie Makepeace and the spire.'

Val looked at me over her spectacles. 'And, therefore, Jay?'

'Yes. And they had smallpox back then, not to mention bubonic plague—'

'I thought you were thrilled at the prospect of time travel?'

'I am, but it might perhaps benefit from a little forethought. If Jay's in the sixteenth century right now, he's on his own.' And it would explain why his phone seemed to have ceased to exist.

Valerie said nothing, but she transferred her penetrating gaze to the Baron's face.

It was his look of bland innocence that made me suspicious.

'You know something about all this, don't you?' I said. 'Did the Court send you to help, or to spy?'

I wanted him to deny it, but he passed a hand over his face and sighed. 'I sometimes have cause to wish you weren't so astute, Ves.' He caught Val's eye and muttered, 'The whole damned lot of you.'

I folded my arms and gave him the death stare. 'Explain.'

'I can't.'

'You can and will.'

'Ves—'

'All that nonsense about the island moving around was misdirection, was it? All right, so it probably is impossible to haul an entire bloody island around but in that case *where is it*?'

Alban gave me a helpless stare.

'Is it three and a half miles off the coast of Scarborough?' I pressed.

'In a manner of speaking.'

'*In which century?*'

'I... Ves, that is genuinely a complicated question to answer.'

'Or in other words, it's *not this one.*'

'It is,' said Alban, and then added, 'in a manner of speaking.'

I stifled an urge to kick him.

Into the icy silence left by the combined efforts of Val and me, he offered: 'I am not here to obstruct you. Honestly.'

'No?' I said.

'Not necessarily,' he amended, and held up his hands when I threatened to explode on the spot. 'The Court is unsure how to proceed, Ves. This is a... it's an unprecedentedly tricky situation. I am to help where I deem it fit and... and see what happens.'

'Which means you are also to hinder if you deem it fit?'

'If it proves necessary, yes.'

'Hinder whom?'

'Ancestria Magicka, definitely. Hopefully not you.'

Hopefully.

I looked him square in the eye. 'Do you know where that island is right now, Alban?'

He met my gaze without flinching. 'I have an inkling, but I am not yet certain. I have some investigating to do, like you.'

'Are you going to share your *inkling*?'

'I can't, at present. Their Majesties have expressly forbidden it. But it pains me to have to say no, Ves.'

'Comforting,' I said tartly. 'Thank you.'

His lips curled in a tiny, unhappy smile. 'You're welcome.'

'We'll find out anyway.'

His smile turned more genuine. 'I would expect nothing less.'

'It's party time,' said Val crisply.

Startled, I checked the time: six o' clock. Just an hour left to get dinner and find a dress. 'Wait,' I said, frowning at Val. 'How do you know about that?'

'How? I was invited.'

'What? Who else?'

'I don't know everybody who got an invitation, but Rob for one. Nell. Indira, Rosalind, Siobhan, Berat, Vincent, Ravindra, Jack, um, rumour has it they even invited Orlando.'

It did not escape my notice that everyone on Val's list (and mine) was either a figure of some authority at the Society, they were particularly experienced or specialised in their field, or they possessed rare talents of one sort or another. 'They're trying to swipe more of our best people, aren't they?'

'Milady drew the same conclusion, but I don't think they'll get very far with most of us.'

Nobody mentioned Miranda.

The Baron stood up. 'Time to get something to eat?' he said, looking at me.

Part of me wanted to be petulant and tell him to get stuffed, but it was a small part. And since we were no longer able to wander down to the cafeteria for dinner... 'All right,' I said, grudgingly.

He looked, politely, at Val, but she waved us off. 'I'll see you at Ashdown.'

The Baron offered me his arm, which I took with a sniff of disdain.

'You've a good indignant face,' he said, and that damned twinkle was back in his eyes. 'Had some practice?'

'Thanks to the likes of you, yes.' I refused to be charmed out of my displeasure just yet. Maybe after I'd been fed.

'Ouch,' he said with an exaggerated wince.

'You deserved that.'

'I did.'

THE BARON AND I arrived at Ashdown Castle slightly early. He had certainly known about the party in advance, for he had come prepared, and changed into a delicious deep blue dinner suit while I slipped into my favourite slinky evening gown, a wine-red satin confection (and changed my hair to match: auburn bordering upon burgundy). Alban drove us, utilising some of his enviable Troll Roads, I think, for we made suspiciously excellent time.

I had heard nothing from Zareen, and was left to assume that she, too, would meet us there.

They really had sent out a lot of invitations, for when we swung smoothly into the driveway at Ashdown Castle we were met by the sight of at least fifty cars already parked. The grassy grounds had been turned into a giant car park for the evening, event-style, as though they were expecting nearer five hundred guests than fifty. They had also disabled most of the enchantments which protected the place from unwanted incursions. No concealments remained, no shields, no discouragements of any kind.

'Serious business,' I remarked, taken aback.

'They're planning to cause a stir,' agreed Alban.

He offered his arm as we got out of the car, and I was glad to take it. We walked briskly up to the castle (carefully as well, in my case — heels on grass is always a risky proposition). The scale of the event and the mystery surrounding it made it clear that this was to be no ordinary party, and I was alert for signs of trouble or intrigue as we made our way to the entrance.

Well, the next thing I noticed was that Ashdown Castle had undergone something of a facelift.

13

I HAD PAID A visit to Ashdown Castle before, only a few weeks past. On that occasion, the place had been half a ruin, with parts of its roofs fallen in, glass missing from the windows, walls tumbling down — a wreck, in short. What a pity, too, for it was a large, rambling old place, five centuries old, with appealing higgledy-piggledy architecture all built from unusual brown brick.

The several sloping roofs were all intact, now. The windows glittered with bright, new glass, every rickety wall had been rebuilt or stabilised, and there had even been some cleaning done to its decorative stone embellishments. How they had achieved so much in so short a space of time was beyond me to imagine; I could only gape in astonishment, and marvel again at just how much money these people had to throw around.

'I really, *really* want to know who's funding this lot,' I muttered to the Baron.

'Yes,' he replied, grimly. 'We were thinking the same thing.'

By *we* I supposed he meant himself and Their Majesties. It wasn't just the money, either. They behaved with the splendid insouciance of people who think that laws are beneath them, and are confident of there being no conceivable way any unpleasant consequences could ever be brought to bear for breaking them. I'd wondered before how many connections they had in advantageous places, especially since Lord Garrogin's duplicity had come to light.

Probably that had occurred to Their Majesties, too.

Our invitations were accepted at the door by a pair of young women in blue uniform robes — or mine was, anyway. The Baron needed no invitation. He had only to announce himself and his eminence did all the work (with a little help from his best and most charming smile, perhaps). The girls on the door looked thrilled as they waved him in. Was it because he was handsome, or because his presence here was another coup for Ancestria Magicka?

In the great hall — whitewashed walls inside, high ceiling, remarkable painted murals depicting forest scenes — we found a large number of our fellow guests already milling about, many of them with champagne glasses in hand.

We also found Zareen, loitering near the door, with George Mercer in tow. He wore a black tuxedo; she was devastating in a slim column of a black dress, her eye make-up dramatic.

'Half the Society's coming,' she hissed as she drew us aside. 'They've invited *everyone*.'

'So I learned from Val. You wouldn't happen to know why, would you?'

We both looked at George Mercer, who had the grace to look uncomfortable.

'They're looking to expand,' said Zareen in disgust. 'At our expense, obviously.'

The same conclusion Milady and I had reached in our separate deliberations, but I was no longer certain that was all that was going on. There was too much show, the party was too big, the guests too varied. What Zareen had said was probably true enough, but what other motive lurked behind all this effort and expense?

'I'd like to know where Jay is,' I said to George, as pleasantly as I could manage considering that I wanted to choke the information out of him with my bare hands.

He grunted. 'You'll find out.'

'Once we've given you the information you want, you mean?' I was ready to do that if it meant getting Jay back.

But Mercer rolled his eyes. 'No.'

I thought Zareen was looking a bit shame-faced. Had she already spilled everything?

She caught my look, and sighed. 'They know all about that bloody island already, all right?'

'They do?' That shed some interesting new light on things. '*All* about it?'

'As much as we know, anyway.'

Mercer, to my interest, looked like he wanted to say something, but he hesitated and Zareen swept on. 'Last recorded position off the coast of Scarborough, vanished since to an undiscovered location.'

He was definitely looking shifty. 'Do you also have an inkling as to where?' I said — politely, I swear!

The man sighed, ran a finger around the collar of his shirt as though it was choking him, and walked off, muttering something about a drink.

Zareen's smile grew satisfied.

'What was that?' I asked.

'Nothing,' she said, but then amended that to: 'Mission almost accomplished.'

'What mission?'

'My secret George Mercer mission.'

'Does it have anything to do with getting Jay back?'

'Sort of.'

I gave up. I'd always known that Jay and Zareen did not altogether get along, but I hadn't expected to find her so unmoved by his mysterious plight. Remonstrating with her was useless. I walked away.

The Baron leaned down to whisper in my ear. 'I think that she has not had the success she was hoping for with Mr. Mercer, but is embarrassed to admit it.'

Hmm. Was she embarrassed or just hopping mad? Either way, uttered in his smooth, calm tones, the idea sounded reasonable, and some of my irritation and dismay dissipated. He was probably right.

I came to a dead halt halfway across the hall, because a familiar figure approached from the other side of the room: an extremely tall figure, clad in robes. 'Lord Garrogin's here?'

The Baron looked about as pleased to see him as I was. 'Bloody cheek,' he muttered.

I was better pleased to see Rob and Nell there, and Val arrived shortly afterwards. I didn't see Miranda, though I was on the watch for her.

I began to feel bad about turning my back on Zareen like that. I knew she was in a difficult position between the Society and George Mercer, and could hardly be blamed for having slightly confused loyalties. She would be doing her best. I ought to be a better friend.

But when I turned to go back to her, she was not where we had left her a few minutes before. It took me a few seconds to locate her among the mass of sumptuously clad guests; they were as curious about the castle as I was. A ceaseless flow of party-goers streamed from door to door, disappearing into the depths of the building and coming back again, probably in search of more champagne.

I would join them in exploring before long, but first... ah, there was Zareen, in a corner by herself. She had her eyes closed. As I drew nearer, I saw that she was pressed into the walls, one hand laid palm-flat against the pale plaster. Her face was pale and drawn in that way I was beginning to dread seeing.

I approached carefully, wary of startling her. 'Zar?' I said softly.

Her eyes snapped open. They were only half filled in with black, yet, but the colour was spreading into the whites. 'Yes. You know the...' she trailed off as Alban came up beside me.

'Carry on,' I murmured. 'The Baron's all right.'

'I'd rather not.' The look in Zareen's eyes too nearly resembled fear for my liking, so I was glad when Alban took this in good part, and moved quietly away again.

'The Greyer cottage,' Zareen continued, pitching her voice lower. 'And how George and Katalin almost beat us to it.'

'Yes.'

'We thought they were trying to purloin the services of Wester, and maybe one of the Greyers, for themselves. And we were right.'

'But you exorcised them, so that put paid to that plan.'

'But it didn't. It's something George said earlier today...' Her eyes fluttered shut again, and she visibly swallowed. I couldn't imagine what was going on in her mind at that moment. 'There are more Waymasters like Wester. Millie Makepeace, for one, and George claims they've another tame one in some building somewhere, he wouldn't say in any more detail. But I think that's not the half of it. You've been here before, haven't you?'

'Once, a few weeks ago.'

'Notice anything different about it?'

'Only everything.' I told her about the castle's formerly derelict state.

'Building works,' Zareen whispered, and said hoarsely: 'Yes. There are at least seven spirits loose in here.'

'*Seven?*'

She nodded. 'Perhaps more, I am having trouble separating them. Some of them are... *really* not happy.'

I've a notion my face turned as paper-white as Zareen's. Seven spirits, most or all of them conveyed here with or without their consent, their bones sealed into newly rebuilt floors or walls. Possibly more than seven. 'Are they all Waymasters?'

'At least two of them are. One is called Bonnie Bishop. I know this because she keeps shrieking her name at me. She was a healer in a village called Combe Greening. Edward Visser kept a charms and cantrips shop in Amesbury. Harriet Theale was a vicar's wife in a parish called Bodwell. Two of them are talking in languages I cannot understand and the rest are just— I can't distinguish.' Zareen gripped her head, her eyes wide and staring now, and black from edge to edge. 'Eight,' she said with forced calm. 'Toby McNeal, Kinross. Waymaster and baker.'

'Zar.' I took hold of her hands, and tried to make her look at me. 'Zar, stop. Where is this coming from? You were fine a few minutes ago.'

'They were silent until a few minutes ago. I didn't know they were there. They woke up, all at once.'

That boded poorly. The party was just getting underway, pretty much everyone was here who was going to be here, and now the ghosts in the walls woke up?

'I need George,' said Zareen shakily, and tried to pull free of me.

I hung onto her. 'We'll find him together. Come on.'

Baron Alban, bless him, had not been oblivious to this. He was at my side in an instant as I set off across the hall, supporting Zareen. He took up a position on her other side, his bulk helping to shield her from unwanted attention, and with his superior height he was the first to spot George Mercer slipping through a half-concealed door at the back of the hall.

We followed.

'Stranger Arts?' murmured the Baron to me as we passed through the door.

'Mm.'

He looked more sympathetic than repulsed, and duly went up yet another notch in my estimation.

'George!' gasped Zareen. 'Stop. Please.'

For a moment I thought he would ignore her, but to his credit he slowed, and turned around. He looked every bit as bad as Zareen, if not worse, his face chalk-coloured and his eyes pitch. Shadows crept across his skin, giving him a chilling, cadaverous air. 'I *told* you to stay away,' he said, his voice rasping like rusted metal.

'And that's why I came. You're holding them here, aren't you? You've got to let them go.'

'I can't.'

'George. They're tearing themselves to pieces.'

'They'll tear *me* to pieces if I try it.'

'If they do, so be it.' Zareen was ice-cold. 'You should never have done this.' She swallowed, choked, and added: 'Nine. Bob Malley, Kellswater. He wants to go home, George.'

George's reply, whatever it might have been, was drowned by a sudden blare of music from the hall. No, it was not coming from the hall, or not only from the hall. It was coming from everywhere at once. I might have suspected a complicated speaker system, except that the music — strings and trumpets, with something of the fanfare about it — seemed to explode from the very walls. Then came a woman's voice. 'Ladies and gentlemen, welcome to Ashdown Castle! Ancestria Magicka is delighted to make your acquaintance. Your presence is kindly requested in the main ballroom for the first of several scintillating surprises, so make haste! We begin in five minutes!'

A look of utter horror flashed across George's face, prompted by... what?

'Ten,' said Zareen. 'Felicity Bennett, Ivybridge. Seamstress.'

'Right,' I said, straightening my spine. 'Zar, you need to stop this. Shut them off. They'll drive you insane, and there is nothing you can do for them at this moment.'

Zareen nodded ready acquiescence, to my relief — but then she shuddered so violently she almost fell to the floor. The Baron and I caught her between us.

I stared flintily at George, my heart pounding. 'What is going on here?'

But I was too late. He gave the same tearing shudder as Zareen, but while she had weathered it, George did not. His eyes rolled up and he collapsed.

14

The ballroom was already crowded by the time we arrived. We were among the last to squeeze our way into the vaulted chamber, and there was barely space enough for us. I was relieved to find Rob just inside the door, apparently on the watch for us. 'Is she all right?' he said at once, already reaching for Zareen.

'I'm *fine,*' said Zar, and she was recovering by then, though still rather weak. She straightened up, shaking me off, and lifted her chin. Her eyes, thankfully, were normal again.

Mercer had revived after a couple of minutes, but refused to come with us. He'd staggered off into the bowels of the castle, and we had let him go.

Rob nodded. 'Trouble?'

Zareen gave him a quick account of the ten (or more) Waymasters she had sensed locked into the walls, and I watched as Rob's face grew very grave. 'Ten Waymasters ought to be enough to move a castle, wouldn't you think?' he said when she had finished.

'Fair chance of it.'

A small stage occupied the far end of the ballroom, raised up very high. A smattering of applause broke out as a woman strode out onto it, dressed in a dazzling gown that glittered like the night sky. When her identity became clear, the applause became thunderous.

I was too astonished to move.

'That's Fenella Beaumont,' I hissed.

Let me tell you about the Beaumonts. They were a powerful magickal family some few hundred years ago, and Ashdown Castle had been their principal seat for many generations. But they'd withered away down the ages; their powers and their fortune had declined at about equal rates, and most of them had died out. Fenella Beaumont was one of only two surviving members of the family — and she had not been seen or heard from in so long, some had begun to say she, too, was dead.

Well, she wasn't. With her silvery hair swept up in a fairy-tale style and her still slender figure encased in sparkling velvet, she was causing a sensation up on the stage.

'Welcome to my ancestral home!' she said, when at last the applause began to die down. 'It is a pleasure to see my beloved Ashdown Castle not only restored to its former glory but also hosting such a distinguished set of guests. I hope you have all been suitably supplied with champagne?'

A roar of assent.

'Her home?' I whispered to Rob. 'Ancestria Magicka bought this place last year.'

'From Everett Beaumont,' said Rob. 'Her uncle.'

Everett Beaumont was famously destitute, hence the appalling state of disrepair the castle had fallen into — and its sale. Fenella Beaumont was as broke as the rest of them, so what was she doing up there in a designer gown, diamonds flashing at her ears and throat?

'Let me introduce you to Ancestria Magicka,' Fenella was saying, flashing a charming smile. 'Many have called for a progressive, forward-thinking organisation for the magickal among us. Many have chafed against the needless restrictions laid down by our sisters and brothers at the Ministry, among the Courts of the Fae, and the many other establishments tasked with the protection and preservation of our kind. And they do fine work, do they not? But it isn't enough.' Fenella began to pace back and forth across the stage. A good move, I had to admit: she had a fluid, graceful stride, and the sparkle sent up by her gown and her jewels had a nearly mesmeric quality. 'It isn't enough to be safe. It isn't enough to be careful. If we want to regain what we've lost, well, somebody has to take risks!'

She stopped, and looked seriously out over her audience. 'We all know what we've lost, don't we? Our arts have declined with every passing century, smothered by the relentless rise of modernity and technology. Even the greatest of our living practitioners has nothing to compare with the witches and sorcerers, the waymasters and necromancers, of ages long past. This isn't right. Where will we be in another hundred years? Another two centuries? Will there be anything of magick left?

'And that isn't all. My friends, my colleagues, we have lost far more than any of you realise. More than that: it has been taken from us, hidden from us. You are all being lied to, every single day, by those you look up to. Our leaders have swaddled us in comforting half-truths and outright lies, all in the name of safety! Of miserable *caution*! In so doing, they collude in our destruction.

'We cannot go on this way.'

She paused here for effect, and you could have heard a pin drop in that room. Some of the people near me did not even seem to be breathing. The woman had presence, I'd give her that. 'A year ago today, I founded Ancestria Magicka,' continued Fenella. 'To fight back. To find a new way forward. To reclaim our lost heritage. I see a brighter, more magickal future ahead and it is my dearest wish to share it with all of you.'

The tension in the room became palpable, and I sensed that the first of those "scintillating surprises" was about to be dropped on us. (If we weren't counting the involvement of Fenella herself. Even the purchase of Ashdown Castle, of all places, hadn't tipped me off about her).

'We may have left the best of our arts behind us, but what if I told you they are *not* lost? What if I told you there is a way to get them back?'

It was my turn to stop breathing. I clutched the Baron's arm so hard it must have hurt, but he didn't move. His attention was riveted upon Fenella Beaumont.

'Look at our world,' said Fenella. 'Half drained of magick, and what little is left must be hidden away. *We* are forced to hide in the shadows. Why, there is an entire Ministry devoted to no other purpose! But why? Why must we hide? Why has magick declined?

'It is claimed that this is a natural and inevitable process — that there is nothing we could have done to slow or halt this decline. That as the world progressed, as technology improved, we and our magick must necessarily be left behind.

'This is false. It is through our own poor choices, our own weaknesses, that modern magick has arrived at this condition. We, and our ancestors, have betrayed everything we have, everything we are, and we continue to do so, day by day. But it doesn't have to be this way.' Fenella stood dead centre of the stage, now, staring out at the audience. She stood tall and proud and majestic, glittering with magick, her eyes alight with fervour; every word she uttered struck me deeply. 'What we have broken, we can mend. We can! And we will!

'How do I know this? Because, my friends, I have seen the proof with my own eyes. Some of those around you have seen it. I have travelled far beyond the borders of Britain. I have travelled far beyond the borders of this world. And I have seen another Britain. *Another world.* One where magick has *not* declined. A world where magick and its practitioners co-exist, peacefully and without conflict, alongside the very same technologies we enjoy in our own reality.'

She was obliged to pause, here, for the ballroom was by then in uproar. I felt like screaming myself. 'What the bloody *hell*?' I gasped. 'What nonsense is this?'

Baron Alban alone had neither moved nor spoken. He just looked at me.

'It's true? It cannot be.' I was shaking all over, I wasn't sure why. Shock? Horror? Awe? I wrapped my arms around myself and took a steadying breath, though it was difficult to muster a state of calm when everyone around me was losing their wits. 'Explain?' I said beseechingly.

'Later.' The Baron looked back at Fenella. 'Methinks the lady isn't finished with us yet.'

He was right. Fenella raised her voice to shout above the tumult. 'I see scepticism in many faces!' she shouted. '*Lies,* I hear you call! It is a difficult idea to believe, is it not? It has been hidden from us, hidden by our own leaders, our own guiding lights. Well, the time for secrets has passed. I bring you truths, and I shall prove that this is no lie.' Her lips curved in a saucy smile. 'How, you ask?

'Why don't I just... show you?'

With splendid theatricality, most of the lights went out, leaving the ballroom in an atmospheric gloom.

And then, too many things happened at once.

Zareen, at my elbow, began abruptly to babble, six or eight voices at once streaming from her lips. Her eyes had gone solid black again, and every muscle in her body was rigid. Her voices rose to a screaming pitch and she clapped her hands over her ears as though to shut something out; her gaze, locked on mine, was wide and desperate.

She collapsed.

'Zar!' I fell to my knees beside her, but there was nothing I could do. She lay shuddering uncontrollably, still babbling in an endless stream of words, her hands clutching helplessly at me.

Then George Mercer was there. He looked little better himself, and his lips moved in concert with Zareen's, uttering the same words which poured still from her mouth. But he bent and hauled her up, steadying her somehow. They clung to one another.

The ground began to shake.

'We're going somewhere,' I gasped, and almost fell as the earth gave a convulsive shudder beneath my feet. A dull roar began as the ancient bricks of Ashdown Castle rattled and shook, as though an earthquake passed through.

'We're going a long way,' said Alban grimly, and I was grateful when he took hold of me, for with his superior weight and bulk he was a lot more stable than I was. I clung to him like he was a tree in a storm and shut my eyes. How did I really feel, in that moment? Terrified, appalled — but afire with excitement, because, good gods, if Fenella spoke the truth... I had no words to express the impact her revelation would have upon everything I knew and cared for.

Rob surged out of the crowd. His dark hair was dusted white with fallen plaster and he had a shield up, a field of magickal energy which flickered darkly around him as he moved. 'Ves!' he bellowed. 'Where's Val?'

I pointed in the direction I'd last seen her, though who knew if she was anywhere near that spot anymore.

'Take care of Zareen!' he shouted, and plunged into the crowd in, hopefully, Val's general direction.

I summoned a shield of my own, taking care that it encapsulated Zareen (and George) and the Baron as well as me. Rob was right: at this rate, Fenella's mad scheme would bring the roof down on us.

The roar of rumbling brick and stone grew louder still, the earth rocked wildly under another tearing shock, and then — then we were gone, hauled bodily through space like the worst of all rollercoasters. Dizziness overwhelmed me, and Alban too, for we went tumbling to the ground and lay there stunned as the world broke into whirling pieces and faded away.

It seemed a long time later when the tremors stopped at last, and the ground ceased to shudder and buckle beneath us. I opened my eyes, tentatively, to find my shield still intact around the dishevelled little group of us, toppled like bowling pins.

'Are we alive?' I croaked.

'Breathing,' said Alban from about three inches away. The pale bluish tint to his skin had developed more of a greenish air, but otherwise he looked hale. He managed, somehow, to smile at me.

Zareen and George were twined tightly together not far from where I lay. Both appeared to be breathing, which was good enough for me at that moment. With a groan, I hauled myself to my feet, and looked around.

The roof had not come down, but plenty of plaster had. Ancestria Magicka's guests were liberally dusted with it, their splendid evening attire nicely ruined. Nobody appeared hurt, or not more than a little. All about me, dazed guests were struggling to their feet.

'Any idea where we are?' I muttered to the Baron.

'Some,' he said. 'Let's find out.'

I looked at Zareen, but she waved a hand weakly at me. 'Go,' she whispered hoarsely, and her lips quirked in a tiny smile. 'Save yourselves...'

I rolled my eyes, and held out a hand to her. 'Come on. Don't you want to see this vision of magickal marvels?'

'*I* do,' she said, and began to shiver. 'My legs don't, and I'm really not sure about my stomach.'

George dragged himself up and stood there for a moment, swaying slightly. When he did not fall, he held out his hand to Zareen. 'We're okay.'

'Speak for yourself.' But she rallied and got herself up somehow. Her eyes were still coal-black, which I tried not to notice, and a trickle of drying blood marred the blanched skin beneath her nose. At least they had both stopped babbling.

I kept the shield up as we left the ballroom. Fortunately we had maintained a station near the rear door, and few people yet stood between us and the questionable safety of the outdoors. Our pace was slow, and I became aware of several hitherto undiscovered bruises as we staggered through the corridors of Ashdown Castle to its main doors. They were closed, but they swung slowly open as we approached, and fresh air rushed in. I took a great, grateful lungful of it.

The sun was up, and it should not have been, for darkness had fallen by the time Fenella began her spectacular speech. We had somehow gone back (or forward) to the middle of the afternoon, or thereabouts, and that fact caused a violent fluttering in my stomach — part excitement, part anticipation, part terror.

'What the fuck is going on,' muttered Zareen, and I agreed whole-heartedly with the sentiment, for beyond the doors of the castle was a sight both unfamiliar and unfathomable.

A sandy beach strewn with stones stretched before us, and beyond that came the deep blue glitter of a sunlit sea. A cliff rose in jagged stages to a height of some hundred feet, a winding roped-off pathway snaking its leisurely way up to the top. Little houses were tucked into nooks and corners at intervals up the cliff, and their architecture was mostly of a type I recognised: timber-frames, whitewashed walls, steeply gabled roofs covered in thatch. But one or two were odd. It took me a moment to realise that their pale, pearly walls were built from starstone, and they bore some of the same whimsical features as Melmidoc's Striding Spire.

One of them even had a short, round tower of almost identical design.

My gaze made its way slowly up this bizarre and inexplicable cliff and when I at last took in what lay at the very top, I received another shock, for there was Melmidoc's own spire. It stood casually at the edge of the cliff, a pale, elegant shape against the deep blue sky, and just to round the day off nicely there was a familiar figure coming out of the door at its base.

Jay looked down at the group of us huddled on the beach, shading his eyes against the sun. Then, curse him, he gave us a cheery wave.

'What,' I said slowly, 'the *fuck* is going on.'

Jay beckoned.

'Right, then,' I said, squaring my shoulders. 'All ready for another dose of strange beyond all reason?'

'Bring it on,' said Alban.

15

'You made it!' said Jay, smiling, once we had finally crawled our way to the top of the cliff.

Fortunately for him, I was a bit too out of breath from the climb to make any immediate reply. I occupied myself instead with gazing out over the water. A town was distantly visible on the horizon, but I was insufficiently familiar with Scarborough to be able to tell whether or not it looked the same.

'Uh huh!' said Zareen brightly and added, with deceptive casualness, 'And where exactly have we made it to?'

'Oh, the fifth Britain. This is Whitmore, centre of magickal government for the North.' He eyed me in my slinky evening gown and added, 'Nice dress.'

Faced as he was with four identically pole-axed expressions, I suppose he could be forgiven the smug smile. 'There's lots to tell,' he conceded.

'Wait,' said Baron Alban. 'The *fifth* Britain? Five?'

'Yes,' said Jay. 'There are —'

'*Five?*' Zareen and I yelped in concert.

'Well—' said Jay.

'*Five* worlds like ours,' I said, and folded my arms. 'You cannot be serious, Jay.'

'I'm not,' he said, and folded his arms right back at me. 'There are nine.'

Nine that are known, came Melmidoc's voice. The door to the Starstone Spire stood open, and we had all paused only a few feet away. *Many scholars believe that there are more yet to be discovered.*

Zareen threw up her hands and took a step back, signalling her incapacity to cope with the conversation just then. I didn't blame her. George Mercer hadn't said a word; he stood a little apart from the rest of us, stony-faced and silent. From the look of him, I suspected his behaviour was prompted in large part by simple exhaustion. Zareen's too, probably.

'Which scholars?' said Alban.

Whitmore is also a centre of learning, said Melmidoc. *Academics from more than one of the nine have gathered here. Even one or two from* your *Britain, Baron.*

'Well, this is...' Alban left the sentence unfinished, and looked helplessly at me.

'How many did you know about?' I said shrewdly, for he alone had been little surprised by the general substance of Fenella's speech.

'Three are known to the Court. Not, I think, including this one.'

Considering the unique obstacles posed by your particular Britain, that is a respectable achievement, Melmidoc remarked.

'Thank you.' The Baron's voice was wintry.

'How are there nine?' I put in, my mind reeling. 'Are they all the same? Did they all come into being at the same time? How did you get here — what is this island — what became of the Whitmore of our Britain — what did you mean about the magickal government for the North — the *North*? Is there a separate one for the South? Why? Is that the fifth Scarborough over there? I—'

Peace, interrupted Melmidoc, and I stopped gabbling with a gulp.

'Sorry. But when we've finished with those questions I have about two thousand more.'

Melmidoc gave a dry chuckle. *Questions are the product of an enquiring mind, and should never be apologised for. Let me begin with the first. How are there nine? Multiple theories upon that point have been proposed, but none have yet been proved beyond all doubt. They are not thought to have come into being all together, but that, too, is the subject of debate.* Melmidoc's dry voice warmed with enthusiasm as he continued. *I will be happy to hold a more detailed discourse with you upon those topics, should you like to hear about the leading theories. Now then, how do we get here? It is a sideways step, nothing more. Simple in explanation, difficult in practice, for your young friend here has not yet contrived to master the ability despite two days of practice. Perhaps, in your Britain — ours, I should say — it is by now a lost art. I should be sorry to think so. The Whitmore of your Britain sank, I am afraid. Rather an inconvenience to us at the time, but our removal here has turned out very well indeed, for we have been able to build the kind of magickal government in the North of this Britain of which we could only dream under the conditions prevailing in the sixth.*

'That's ours?' I put in. 'The sixth Britain?'

Yes.

'What is the fourth like?'

Of the nine worlds, said Melmidoc patiently, *three are no more, including the one we think of as the fourth. In two, magick has met a permanent death and cannot now be revived at all. Of the four remaining, two have succumbed to fear and irrationality and outlawed magick entirely. That leaves your world, where magick survives in a diminished and hidden capacity, and this one, the fifth Britain, where magick thrives and need never hide.*

I thought briefly of Fenella Beaumont, and Ancestria Magicka. To build so powerful an organisation in a single year, she must have had an equally powerful motive. Was this it? Had she somehow discovered the fifth Britain, a vision of a world where people like us could practice our magicks openly, and with unabated power?

It was a seductive prospect, that I could not deny. But what did she now plan to do?

I hesitate to call a close to this instructive interlude, said Melmidoc, *but was it strictly necessary to bring so large a party hither?*

Startled, I looked down over the cliff. For a little while, I'd forgotten about the rest of Fenella's guests. They had made their way out of the transplanted castle by now and were milling about on the beach — staring around at everything, exclaiming and, in short, looking like a pack of excited tourists.

Which, I suppose, we all were.

'They pose a problem,' I said, and outlined the events of the past few hours — for Jay's benefit as well as Melmidoc's.

And you do not think they are here in good faith?

'In a spirit of happy exploration, with the best of intentions and no nefarious motives in mind? No.'

Then they will be disposed of, said Melmidoc mildly.

'Not chilling at all.' As I watched, Fenella took up a spot partway up the cliff and began, once again, to hold forth. From this height, I could not hear what she was saying, but it involved a fair amount of pointing and gesturing up to the top of the cliff, and over the water to the huddle of buildings clinging to the far shore. I could not see Rob or Val in the mass of people, or any of our folk. Wherever they had gone, it wasn't with Fenella.

'Let's go in,' said Jay, and the door of the spire creaked open a bit wider in invitation. 'I can see we're going to need a cunning plan.'

I stared hungrily over the island of Whitmore, spread before us like a birthday buffet. I had a fierce lust to explore its plethora of shining buildings, their architecture so intriguing a mixture of the familiar and the strange; another spire rose somewhere in the distance, so similar in style to Melmidoc's that it had to be related, and was that Drystan's? Another set of people wandered the narrow streets of the town, similar to and yet different from us in the same way as their homes and shops and offices. What must it be like, to grow up here, live here, work here right out in the open? As part of an organisation known to, and accepted by, every denizen of this world whether magickal or not? What feats were they capable of, that we had forgotten long ago?

But now was not the time, for we had a more pressing problem on our hands: Fenella. I'd have to trust that my opportunity to explore would come soon, if not today. 'What's become of Millie?' I asked as I preceded Jay into the Starstone Spire.

'She's dozing,' he answered, ushering Zareen and George inside. The Baron brought up the rear, uncharacteristically quiet. I wondered just how many questions were buzzing through his mind at that moment, and how many worries. He rewarded my look of enquiring concern with a smile and the barest trace of a wink.

'In the hopes of warding off a beating,' said Jay as we trooped up the stairs, 'I did try to find a way to get word to you, but phones from our Britain don't work here — big surprise — and Millie can't go back and forth all that often. It tires her.'

I am afraid I declined to be pressed into service as a messenger, Melmidoc put in, *though Mr. Patel is tiresomely persuasive. In another day, perhaps two, I would have been dispatched quite against my will, I am sure of it.*

'Ves worries,' said Jay, with a shrug.

She appears to me the very picture of a composed young woman.

'All a lie. Underneath that calm exterior, she's stewing over at least a dozen things.'

I blushed, for this I could not deny. 'Maybe not a dozen...'

'Anyway,' Jay continued, 'I wanted to share. Who wouldn't?' We reached the top of the spire, where the cosy library had once been. The room was still bare in comparison with before, but Jay had acquired a few chairs from somewhere and hauled them in — somehow — and he now collapsed into one. 'It's amazing,' he enthused. 'You have to get a look around, Ves. This is what our world could've been like, if we hadn't screwed everything up.'

'You know,' I said, taking the chair beside his. 'That's more or less exactly what Fenella Beaumont was saying before she kidnapped us all here.'

'Uh huh. And who is she?'

I explained.

Jay looked nonplussed, but he shrugged. 'Never thought I'd be in agreement with Ancestria Magicka, but she's not wrong.'

'No, indeed. But what of it? It's too late to turn our Britain into this one.'

'Is it?' One of Jay's brows went up.

The world shifted under us, but subtly. Melmidoc had moved us, but it came in a smooth, unobtrusive feeling of motion, nothing like Ashdown Castle at all. The effects of practice, I supposed.

'It is,' said Alban. 'Well — it is too late to come out of the shadows. Can you imagine the result if we tried?' He had eschewed the chairs in favour of perching on the windowsill, and he did not look at us as he spoke: his attention was fixed upon the island flying by outside.

'Total uproar,' I said, for I had to agree.

'True,' Jay conceded. 'But all our lost arts? What could we relearn, with help from the fifth?'

'You did not have much luck learning to jump sideways, right?'

Jay rolled his eyes, and slouched disconsolately in his chair. 'I've had only two days to practice. It took more like two years to learn to jump at all, as you put it. If I could stay here—'

'Wait.' I stared, shocked. 'You want to stay?'

Jay avoided my eyes. 'Think about it, Ves. All the things we could learn. All the things we could *do.*'

I had been thinking about it, pretty much without cease ever since Fenella had opened her big mouth and let all these delicious and dangerous secrets come tumbling out. It was, as I have already said, a seductive prospect. 'But.' I rallied, with a struggle. 'This is exactly why we have to go home. We're needed there. We aren't remotely needed here.'

'And we could do our work much better *there* if we've been properly trained *here*. I don't propose to stay forever, Ves. Just long enough.'

'How long is long enough?'

Jay just shrugged.

'Melmidoc,' said the Baron, finally turning around. 'I don't think we should leave that lot roaming around Whitmore for very long. Certainly not without supervision.'

Do not be concerned, said Melmidoc coolly. *They are not unsupervised.*

'Oh?'

Almost every house on Whitmore has its own occupants with my general characteristics, he supplied. *Most have more than one. I am receiving regular reports as to the movements of your friends.*

'Not our friends,' Zareen said coldly.

'Hey,' said George. 'Some of them are mine.'

'Yes, about that?' Zareen threw him a challenging look. 'You need better friends.'

'So you've said.'

I held up a hand to forestall further argument. 'Are you saying every building on the entire island is haunted?' I said to Melmidoc.

Haunted. His dry, aged voice registered amusement. *If you wish to call it by such a term.*

'It's the best I've got,' I apologised. 'I come from the diminished sixth, remember? These things are rare and weird back there.'

Rare and weird. Melmidoc was definitely laughing at me.

'You know what I mean.'

'What are their movements?' interrupted Alban.

At present they are nearing the top of the cliff. They seem to be engaged mostly in pointing at things and saying the word wow *unnecessarily often.*

Tourists.

Which raised an unpleasant prospect for the fifth Britain, for this was what Fenella's decisions would initially condemn them to. Endless trips from starry-eyed magickal tourists. Whitmore awash with wistful and marvelling magickers from the sixth Britain, eager to see and experience every single little thing they could — and to take as much of it back with them as possible.

What's more, Jay would not be the only person who'd try to stay. Far from it. Our own, beloved Britain would be half emptied of magickers by the time the excitement died down, which would only cripple it further.

We had a full-scale emergency on our hands.

16

'LISTEN,' I SAID, AND explained some of this. 'We have to find a way to stop Fenella, or virtually every magicker from our world will try to move here.'

'It may be too late,' said Alban. 'She made a very big, very public announcement about it all, remember? As soon as her people make it home, they'll spread the news far and wide.'

'If they make it home.'

Alban just looked at me.

'What if we could persuade Ashdown Castle to go home without them?'

I do not want them here! said Melmidoc.

'Just for a little while! We need time to talk with Milady, and Their Majesties, and the Ministry, and pretty much every other magickal authority in the sixth Britain-and-be-yond, and figure out how to — uh, deal with this.'

I will not have them here. Melmidoc spoke with a ringing certainty which echoed through the floors and set my teeth on edge.

'Besides,' put in Zareen, 'Ashdown Castle is going nowhere today. You heard Jay. Millie Makepeace is an old hand at this and even she can't world-hop all that often. Those poor, naïve bastards at the Castle aren't even capable of coherent thought right now.'

'So if we can't leave everyone here and we can't ship them home? What's the third option?'

'Scare the living daylights out of them,' said Zareen, flashing what I tend to think of as her batshit crazy smile. 'Tell them it only gets worse, and will, if they ever tell a soul.'

I looked at Zareen in silence, and my mind wandered back to that pamphlet of hers. Just what weird and far from wonderful things had Zareen done in her life?

'What?' she said, when nobody else spoke either. 'We're in the land of haunted houses. Scaring Ancestria Magicka silly would be a piece of cake.'

'But not lastingly effective.' Alban favoured Zareen with one of his grave, serious looks — which, it struck me, were relatively rare. There was so often that lurking twinkle in his eye. 'Fear fades. We need something more durable.'

Zareen acknowledged this point with a gracious nod. Apparently practicality weighed more with her than morality.

Good to know.

'If only there was a way to undo it,' I sighed. 'Fenella's entire announcement. I'm a bit gutted that this wasn't about time travel after all.'

'You don't truly want to travel in time, Ves,' said Jay.

'I do too.'

'Weren't you panicking about smallpox, when you thought Jay was lost in 1789?' said Zareen.

'There's that, but—'

Jay was laughing at me. 'And measles and polio and bubonic plague and a host of other nasties,' he added. 'Then there's all the other problems. Like, we're giants compared to the people of a few centuries ago, we'd stick out like a sore thumb.'

'Maybe not Ves,' said Alban, and the twinkle was back.

I stuck out my tongue at him.

'And you couldn't have cornflower-coloured hair,' said Jay, wisely electing not to join in casting aspersions upon my height. 'Then there's clothes. I know historical costume can be convincing, but only to us. Try making a liripipe hood that'd pass inspection six hundred years ago. There would be a thousand things wrong with it. It would be like people six centuries from now trying to make a passable pair of jeans, armed with about three paintings in oils and exactly no extant examples. Do you think they'd look real to us?'

'Details,' I said, waving all this away.

'And then there's the lawlessness of society, the fact that getting robbed or raped or murdered would be about six thousand times more likely than it is now and there's no police to call, no ambulance to summon—'

'*All right*,' I said, glaring. 'Point made.'

He smiled at me, half apology, half sympathy. 'But aside from all of that, it would be fantastic.'

'Way fantastic.' I went to the window, and feasted my eyes upon the view. Melmidoc had taken us to the top of a tallish hill, and from that vantage point most of Whitmore lay spread before us. Its starstone buildings shone, pearly and faintly blue, in the afternoon sun, the white plaster or smooth grey brick of its less fantastical buildings gleamed, and everywhere I looked I saw the same vague shimmer of latent magick, just like the dells and enclaves at home. I could see why Jay wanted to stay. It would take me a lot less than two days to fall in love with this place.

There may be another way, said Melmidoc, interrupting the flow of chatter that had been rippling back and forth among my friends.

'Another way to what?' I said, turning back to the room.

To undo your inconvenient colleague's announcement.

'She's not— never mind. What are you thinking of?'

It does not matter what came to pass, if no one present happens to remember it.

Baron Alban shifted uneasily. 'That practice is outlawed in the— the sixth Britain, and for good reason.'

What are these good reasons?

'It is impossible to be precise with the amnesiate charm. More memories than just those targeted are lost, which makes it unethical—'

It is impossible for you *to be precise with the charm,* said Melmidoc frostily. *It was not so in my day, and it is not so here.*

Alban blinked, taken aback. 'My apologies,' he said, with his diplomat's graciousness. 'I did not mean to cast doubt upon your skills.'

It can be difficult to grasp that one's own limitations are not shared by all. Melmidoc, clearly, was not ambassador material.

Alban's mouth twitched. 'Regardless, it is difficult to condone the erasing of memories in so large a group of people.'

Then do not. Your friends may, perhaps, think differently.

The Baron looked my way, and must have seen my very different opinion in my face, for he sat once more upon the windowsill with a sigh. I waited for him to speak, but he did not.

'You're in a difficult position,' I said, drifting nearer. 'Their Majesties' authority may not extend to the fifth Britain, nor are the people of Ancestria Magicka any subjects of theirs. But you must still report to them upon our return, and justify your actions, and that makes this hard for you.'

'But?' he said. 'I presume there's one coming.'

'But, I don't have to.'

'Have to what?'

'Play by the rules. Not for now. Jay and Zar and I are officially cut loose and that gives us freedoms—'

'Ethics still apply, Ves!'

'Can you think of a better solution?'

His eyes met mine, and held. 'No,' he grunted at length. 'Of course I can't.'

'Then we'll have to use this one, and if necessary you can blame it all on me.'

He smirked. 'You'll enjoy that when you're languishing in a gaol cell at Mandridore.'

'I am not among their subjects, so they can't imprison me.'

They can try, muttered Melmidoc.

I'd forgotten he had history with the Troll Court.

'The thing is, Ves, when you requested Their Majesties' aid you brought me here in an official capacity. And I have to act as such.'

'All right. What would they do?'

He threw up his hands and physically retreated from me. 'I don't know.'

'Rules have to be broken sometimes, when the need is great enough. Go on, try to tell me this isn't great need. I'm listening.'

I received a stony, silent glare.

'This is why Milady cut us loose,' I continued relentlessly. I realised, distantly, that I was ruining all my chances with the Baron and that stung, but this was too important. I couldn't worry about that. 'These are problems of unprecedented severity and nobody knows how to deal with them. There is no protocol, no rulebook, to cover any of this.'

Alban's lips twisted with something that looked dauntingly like disgust. 'Has it occurred to you?' he asked. 'That Fenella probably started out saying just these kinds of things to herself.'

I flinched at that, but went doggedly on anyway. 'I am not going to turn into Fenella.'

'Fenella probably never meant to turn into Fenella, either.'

'Enough,' snapped Zareen. 'Comparing Ves to that pile of horse manure is absurd, and you know it.'

Alban closed his lips, and said not another word.

For some reason, I found myself looking at Jay. Zareen's notions of morality did not, I was learning, quite stand up to close scrutiny. Much as I appreciated her support, I could not take her ideas as my guide. Jay was another matter. He drove me mad sometimes, clinging stubbornly to the rules in every situation, and for all that he teased me about fretting over consequences, he was every bit as bad in his own way.

'Urgh,' said Jay, his customary glibness unequal to the demands of the situation. 'You're going to make me decide?'

'Nobody cares what I think, I suppose?' said George acidly.

'No,' said I, and Zareen and Jay and the Baron, all at once.

Our Ancestria Magicka interloper subsided back into silence, glowering.

'I won't make you,' I said to Jay. 'You can abstain, if you want to.'

Jay struggled with the issue for about twenty seconds, then sighed. 'The trouble with you, Ves, isn't that you're amoral. You aren't. It's that, for all your flower-coloured hair and your trinkets and your jewels, you're too damned practical. The rest of us will wrestle with the rules and the ethics and the precedents and the expectations surrounding a given course of action for some time before concluding, regretfully, that there aren't any other options that would get the job done nearly so well, or even at all. You go through the same process in three seconds flat, square your shoulders, lift your chin to the sky and get on with it. It's sometimes hard to keep up with you.'

'So that's yes?' I interpreted.

He waved a hand in a vaguely assenting gesture. 'I don't love it any more than the Baron does, but I can't think of a single alternative that doesn't lead to catastrophe.'

'Indeed, no one can.'

'At least *I'm* not getting amnesiated.'

Are not you? said Melmidoc, sounding surprised.

Jay's mouth dropped open. 'What?'

Does not the same logic apply equally to all visitors from the sixth?

'No! We aren't bringing the hordes down on you.'

Ah. I shall take your word for it, shall I?

The problem here was, Jay couldn't absolutely guarantee that we wouldn't. If we took news of this back to our own Britain, and the people to whom we owed allegiance there, what might come of it? We could neither predict nor control the actions of the Society, or the Troll court, or the Ministry. I saw this dawn on Jay by slow degrees, and his face filled with dismay.

Melmidoc must have liked something about him, or he would certainly have turfed Jay back to his own Britain right away. But did that mean he would give Jay, and the rest of us, a free pass?

'Maybe we'll be able to work something out,' I said pacifically. 'But first, Ancestria Magicka, and guests. Melmidoc, what would you need in order to amnesiate the lot of them?'

The forgetting charms are more my brother's speciality than my own, Melmidoc mused. *We will draw them to his spire, and there the work shall be done.*

'And then we'll need a way to get them home again,' I pointed out. 'And quickly, before they have a chance to wander off.'

'The castle won't do,' Zareen warned. 'To be honest, I'll be surprised if that place will ever move again.'

That would be inconvenient, but I couldn't help laughing a bit at the confusion the castle's disappearance would cause. The papers would enjoy that one. Maybe the publicity would be sufficient to distract attention from the various other things we were much more anxious to hide.

'I'll talk to Millie,' said Jay. 'She should be ready to travel soon, and there's just about enough space for everyone.'

'But how do we get them all to the spire, and then from there to the farmhouse?' I had visions of trying to herd a whole partyful of people around like sheep.

Perhaps my brother might be disposed to visit the farmhouse, Melmidoc put in.

'Can he do that?'

The reply was scornful. *Naturally.*

I did not think it was natural to most people in Melmidoc or Drystan's position, but chose not to say so. I'd only receive another round of disdain along the lines of *one's own limitations are not universal,* and considering the extent of their achievements, the Redclover brothers had a right to a degree of arrogance.

'That would be perfect,' I said instead. 'Then all we have to do is shepherd a bunch of excited explorers into the least interesting building on the island and hold them there until Millie gets us all home. Simple.'

'I'm not going home,' Zareen said.

'What?'

'And neither is George.'

17

'*WHAT?*' SAID GEORGE.

'Someone needs to tend to those poor Waymasters. They're frightened and traumatised and I can't just leave them like that. And,' she added, looking at George, 'I'll need your help.'

But— Melmidoc began.

'It's in your best interests to allow it,' said Zareen. 'Unless you want Ashdown Castle occupying beach-space forever.'

You raise a persuasive point, Melmidoc conceded.

'You'll be all right here on your own?' I said. Not that I doubted Zareen's capability, but to be stranded in a parallel world with only George Mercer to help her, and a castle full of broken spirits her only route home, would not be easy on her. And she was already exhausted.

'I'll be fine.'

Then I remembered Melmidoc. He could still travel between the Britains, and could most likely be persuaded to evacuate the pair of them if it proved necessary. He'd probably be delighted to get rid of them.

And in the meantime, it did solve the problem of what to do about the castle, and George Mercer as well.

'Agreed, then,' I said.

'*Not* agreed,' snarled George.

'It's that or a dose of forgetting and a swift ship-off back home.' Zareen was unsympathetic.

'Screw this.' George was out of his chair and halfway to the door before I had time to register that he'd even moved.

The door, however, slammed shut in his face.

'Oh, come *on!*' He hammered on it and delivered it a violent kick, to no avail.

'George.' Something in Zareen's tone arrested my attention, and George's too. He turned slowly around, simmering with anger but attentive.

'Please,' she said. 'I need you.'

I'd never seen Zareen show so much vulnerability before. Her eyes were huge, and for a moment she looked small and defeated.

At first this entreaty did not appear to have any effect on George. He stood, arms-folded, before the door, brow dark with anger, teeth tightly clenched upon words

I hoped he would not utter aloud. But he looked long at Zareen, and at last the anger drained out of him. He shook his head in frustration, and rubbed wearily at his eyes. For a second he looked almost as vulnerable as Zareen, and my heart softened towards him just a little. 'Fine,' he muttered, and leaned heavily against the door. I wondered if he was having trouble staying upright.

Zareen just nodded, but her gaze spoke volumes.

'Right, then,' I said after a moment, when the silence became awkward. 'What about Rob, Val and the others?'

There are a number of people still in the castle, Melmidoc offered.

'Can you see them?'

Not in the sense that you mean. I believe one of them is injured, however.

Shit. 'We'd better check on that.'

'Are we going to have them forget, too?' Jay asked.

Good point. I thought fast. 'Not Rob or Val. The rest, yes.'

Jay's eyebrows rose. 'Harsh, Ves.'

'Perhaps, but the more people retain this particular secret, the greater the chance it'll leak. Can we vouch for every one of them?' Val had named at least ten people from the Society who had received invitations to Fenella's party. I didn't know if they had all chosen to attend, but I knew that half the people on her list were not close acquaintances of mine. I simply didn't know if they could keep their mouths shut.

Jay, of course, could boast only short acquaintance with any of us, so I'd left him with no argument to offer. He merely shrugged.

I looked at Alban. 'Was there anyone else from the Troll Court present?'

'Other than Garrogin? I don't think so.'

'Not caring about Garrogin.'

He smiled faintly. 'Nor I.'

I felt something nosing at my leg, and looked down.

A tiny hound waved its tail at me. It had sunny-yellow fur, an enormous nose, and a single horn protruding from its furry forehead.

'*Pup?*' I gasped, disbelieving. It couldn't be the same one, could it? My own little friend, taken away with Miranda when she left?

Dwina, said Melmidoc in mild reproof. *Pray do not inconvenience our guests.*

No, of course it wasn't the same one.

I took a moment to check that my valuables were still in places like around-my-neck and circling-my-wrist and not, say, in the mouth of the adorable creature staring up at me with deceptive innocence. They were.

'Are there a lot of these hounds about?' I asked.

I am embarrassed to confess that they have proved much more fertile than we ever anticipated. Indeed, they have become more and more so... There is now a large population of them across Whitmore.

Or in other words, they were reaching pest proportions.

That explained why they kept wandering into cottages and farmhouses and ending up in our Britain.

I stooped to pat Dwina, pleased she'd chosen to show up at that moment. It reminded me of my priorities.

I might consent to leave the place without Zareen, but there was no conceivable way I was leaving without my pup.

'Did we come up with a way to get everyone into the farmhouse?' I asked aloud.

We did not, Melmidoc answered. *But I did. You may leave it to me.*

MELMIDOC TOOK US DOWN from the peak shortly afterwards, parking his beautiful spire on the edge of the cliff once more. We emerged into late afternoon sun, which instantly prompted so huge a yawn from me that I felt embarrassed. It occurred to me that the time back in the sixth

Britain must be at least four in the morning; no wonder I was tired. Hopping between worlds, that was next-level jetlag.

Millie's farmhouse loitered casually at the end of a short, narrow street otherwise lined with rather smaller timber-framed houses. As we approached, I received the impression that she was trying to look inconspicuous (do not ask me how a farmhouse contrives to look ostentatiously inconspicuous; I haven't a hope of explaining anything so absurd). She wasn't getting very far with it.

Her door flew open at Jay's approach, with such vigour as to send it slamming against the wall with a terrific *thunk*. I took it as the building equivalent of a huge smile. *Jay!* she boomed joyfully, and the floor shook. *Come back, come back, I have been so lonesome without you.*

I wondered idly what it was about Jay that people took such a fancy to him. Odd types, too. Last week it had been the dragon Archibaldo, who was still campaigning for Jay's instalment as Mayor of Dapplehaven. This week, a psychotic haunted house with pretty manners and a taste for striped furniture. And even Melmidoc seemed to have a soft spot for him, though I judged he would never admit it. What next?

'Reminds me,' I whispered to Jay as we (Jay, the Baron and I) trooped through the farmhouse's front door. 'Why did you make me wait, when you first went in here?'

Was it my imagination or did he look a bit sheepish?
'Erm, no reason.'

'Tell.'

He sighed. 'I wanted to be sure it was safe.'

'For what?'

'Well, for you.'

Huh?

'What made you think it might not be?' I asked.

He shrugged. 'These haunted houses have their... quirks. Don't they?'

'Hey. Just because she's a homicidal maniac doesn't mean—'

I like that, interrupted Millie. *One little putative murder and people call you a maniac!*

'Sorry,' I muttered.

The temperature in the house grew noticeably colder.

'Quite right,' said Alban, barely controlling the smile that tugged at his lips. 'It takes at least three before the title's deserved.'

Three at least! My uncle was a maniac. We all knew. Four neat little deaths to his credit, and they never caught him. But me! The house gave a great, windy sigh that rattled the windows and set the doors to swaying on their hinges.

Jay patted the nearest wall. 'Most unfair.'

Inside, the house was an odd mix of styles. Some of it looked unchanged since the eighteenth century: her walls were still wainscotted and papered according to tastes two hundred years gone, and she had a fondness for the ornaments and knick-knacks that had graced many a mantelpiece or tea-table in that bygone age. But when I mentioned her taste for striped furniture, I meant that the results were mixed. She had chaise-longues clad in blue-and-white striped silk (tasteful), candy-striped rugs on her floors (a bit less so), and a tall, zebra-striped arm-chair in faux leather (most definitely not). I wondered where she had acquired the latter.

'Millie,' said Jay, taking a seat in that same zebra-pat-terned chair and patting the arm. 'We're here to ask your help.'

You have my attention.

'Are you feeling ready to travel?'

Anywhere with you. The house warmed up again with these words, and a balmy breeze drifted through from somewhere.

The poor girl had a real crush.

Jay looked quickly at me, and gave a slight cough. 'That's wonderful. Will you mind if we take a few other people along with us?'

'These people?'

'And, um, one or two others.'

'About a hundred others,' put in the Baron, with a wink at me. I couldn't disagree. If Millie was going to take exception to the sheer numbers of people involved, better we know that now.

A hundred! Oh, Mr. Patel, is it to be a ball?

Jay blinked, disconcerted, but he couldn't miss the ring of enthusiasm in Millie's words. 'Well... yes, actually it is. They'll all be dressed up and here to party.'

I never got to go to a ball, Millie said sadly. *There was to be a ball at my uncle's but unluckily I was hanged first.*

'How unfortunate,' said Alban, somehow managing to sound sympathetic in spite of his obvious desire to laugh.

It was, because I had the perfect gown! White silk, all trimmed about with lace and real pearls! My aunt had it made up for me in town.

'That sounds lovely,' I said.

They buried me in it.

It fell to Alban to step smoothly into the awkward silence that followed. 'A splendid ball, then, to make up for it all? And perhaps you shan't mind escorting the guests home again afterwards.'

I shall dance with Mr. Patel.

Jay's eyes grew very wide.

With that settled, we set out to return to the castle. Zareen and George had gone on ahead of us, and with Millie's consent gained it was time for Melmidoc to begin the process of rounding up the intruders Fenella had brought. As we stepped smartly back down the narrow street towards the cliff path leading below, nothing much seemed to happen, though we passed one or two over-excited people in evening dress who could only have been some of Fenella's guests.

Then the aged oak front door of a nearby house flew open in a gesture most inviting, and — no word of a lie — a dulcet light beckoned from within. There was even a little burst of strings music coming from inside, with a choir of voices raised in heavenly song. It looked, quite literally, like the gates to paradise.

I drifted that way.

'Ves,' said Alban warningly.

'Mm?' The music drew me, and the light and the warmth and — oh my, there was a heavenly aroma, too. Peaches and strawberries, honey and cake fresh from the oven...

I arrived at the door.

'*Ves.*' It was Jay that time, catching at my arm.

'I'm going in.'

'Don't be—' he broke off, and his grip on my arm went slack as he stared dreamily into the light. The spell had hold of both of us, and we advanced step by step, half in a trance.

'Ves, wait!' Alban's voice, but it reached my ears as though from very far away.

We went through the door. The flaring light engulfed us in a gentle rosy radiance; my lungs filled with heady, tantalising scents of fruit and wine; the heavenly music flared — and then, abruptly, cut off.

18

MR. PATEL! CAROLLED MILLIE. *You are just in time!*

We were back at the farmhouse, ushered through a door so cunningly disguised in all that pearly light that I hadn't noticed it. At least twenty people were already thronging Millie's parlour, and more were arriving all the time, attended by flashes of soft light and bursts of ambrosial music.

'For what?' said Jay, looking about in confusion.

Millie's response was delivered in the form of a burst of song. *A Captain Bold in Halifax, who Dwelt in Country Quarters, seduced a maid who Hanged Herself one morning in her garters!* She accompanied herself on an invisible piano — no, I take that back, it was not invisible. Tucked into one corner of the cosy country parlour was a shabby spinet, the keys of which were cheerily playing themselves.

'Oh, no,' said Jay, briefly closing his eyes.

I judged it was not the first time Millie had taken to song.

His Wicked conscience smited him, he lost his stomach daily! He took to drinking turpentine, and thought upon Miss Bailey. Ohhhhh, Miss Bailey! Unfortunate Miss Bailey!

'Millie...' sighed Jay. 'Please? Stop?'

'It is probably her first public performance,' I murmured to Jay. 'An important moment in any genteel young lady's life. Let her exhibit.'

It cost me something to say as much, for Millie's grasp of tone, melody and key were not as strong as we might all have liked.

Jay sagged against the wall in despair.

Millie sang on.

...A Ghost stepped up to his bedside, and said, 'Behold! Miss Bailey!' As these words floated through the house, I discovered the Baron at my elbow. He raised a quizzical brow at me, and spared a glance for the dejected figure of Jay slumped near the door. 'Stopped for a concert?'

'Absolutely not,' said Jay, coming alive again in a rush. He was out the door and gone in an instant.

We followed.

...and Parson Briggs won't bury me, though I'm a dead Miss Bailey! sang Millie as we pushed our way through the growing throng to the front door.

Which, predictably enough, did not open, though Jay tugged upon it with all his weight. He banged a fist upon it and bellowed: '*MILLIE!*'

The ghostly singing stopped. *You cannot leave yet! There is still another verse!*

'Sing it to me later.'

But— but—

'You can sing me the whole song again later if you like, just let us out.'

I admired his spirit of self-sacrifice.

The front door creaked disconsolately open. Jay dashed through it, followed by the Baron and me, and it slammed shut upon the rest of the hapless guests with a ringing crash. Some few of them had displayed a keen desire to follow our fine example in beating a hasty retreat, but it was not to be.

I spared them a brief moment's sympathy.

'It's lucky she likes you,' I observed as we ran back down the street to the cliff-top. A glimpse of Ashdown Castle was enough to recall me to my purpose. Someone was injured down there, someone from the Society. I hoped Rob was with them. My evening heels were killing me by then, so I took them off, chucked them aside and hastened down the cliff-path in bare feet, making it to the bottom with only one or two small, stinging cuts to show for it. I envied the Baron a little, for not only did he cut a dash in his dark suit and white shirt but he had practical shoes to go along with them.

Ah, well. Such is life.

The great double-doors of Ashdown Castle hung half open. The interior was gloomy in contrast with the golden sunshine outside, and the air was freezing. A hushed atmosphere shrouded the place, though perhaps it just seemed eerily silent compared with the bustle and song of Millie's parlour.

'We had better be quick,' I said as we trooped into the echoing hall. 'It won't take the houses much longer to gather everyone, and Millie can't hold them forever.'

'I wouldn't bet on it,' muttered Jay.

We wasted some time traipsing down corridors and peering into empty rooms without achieving much. All were abandoned, strewn with debris from last night's party that nobody had had occasion or opportunity to clean up. We had ventured all the way to the ballroom before there came a flicker of movement: something, or someone, moved in the shadows. An indistinct shape darted around the corner and disappeared.

I took off in pursuit. 'Wait!' I called. 'We're from the Society. You need to come with us. It's not safe to stay here.' Which was, I feared, the truth. Zareen had called the enslaved Waymasters traumatised and afraid, but five minutes in the castle would have been enough to tell me that for myself. Frigid currents roiled about the floors, doors creaked eerily back and forth, and droplets of water ran down the walls like tears. The deeper we went into the castle, the worse it got.

I rounded the corner and almost slammed into my quarry, who had come to an abrupt stop barely two feet away. A female figure clad in a baggy jumper, hair untidy, head down.

'Ves,' said the figure, and of course it was Miranda.

I struggled for something to say. The best I could manage, in the end, was a cold 'Hello,' while my thoughts spun in agitated circles. Miranda was here after all. What was she doing? What did she want? How could she have the cheek to talk to us?

When she hesitated too long, I said, none too graciously: 'What do you want?'

'I... wanted to apologise.'

I said nothing.

'I don't suppose you'll ever understand.'

'Nope.'

'They offered me so much... think, Ves, how much more I can do for the creatures of Britain! With their resources—'

'If you wanted to switch sides, you should have done it openly. You didn't have to betray us on your way out.'

Miranda's head drooped even lower. 'I know.' She hesitated. 'But it isn't... they aren't our enemies, Ves. I haven't switched sides.'

'I think you'll find that they are. Will you excuse us? We're in a hurry.'

'If you're looking for Val and Rob and the others, they're in the kitchens.'

'Right.' I wheeled and retraced my steps, finding Jay and Alban standing right behind me like a pair of dark vigilantes. Miranda had guts to face the three of us, I had to give her that.

I had to pause. 'Mir, it isn't safe to stay here. You should get out. Up the cliff.' Only half my motive was brutal, I swear. I wanted her herded to Millie's with the rest of her new comrades, but I also didn't want her stranded in a house full of undead Waymasters with newly shredded sanity. She might be a traitor now, but we'd been friends for years.

'Ves. Jay. If there's anything I can do to make up for what I did...'

She was thinking of that tracking spell, I supposed. Fat chance.

Then again...

'Find me my pup,' I said. 'I know she must be here somewhere. I want to take her back with me.'

She made no answer. When I looked round, she had gone.

The three of us went on to the kitchens in silence.

IT WAS VAL WHO was injured. The violence of the castle's transference had, at last, brought parts of the ceiling down. Val, unable to dodge out of the way, had taken a chunk of plaster to the shoulder. Looking at the size of the bleeding gash it had left in her flesh, and the mere few inches that separated the injury and her head, I thanked all our lucky stars that it hadn't been a larger chunk.

She was curled up in her velvet chair, covered in blankets, while Rob hovered about her. There was no sign of anybody else. I took Val's hand and squeezed it, a pressure she returned, though she rolled her eyes at the look on my face. 'I'm fine, Ves.'

'Doesn't look like it.' It really didn't. Rob had found something to bandage the injury, but the wound had bled through, and the bloodied mess of once-white cotton occupied most of her upper arm. I thought how unfair it was. Val rarely left Home, and the one time she did...!

'I'm still breathing, and I plan to keep it up.'

I looked at Rob, who smiled reassuringly. 'She'll be okay. But I want her home as soon as possible. You've got a way out?'

'Will have. Where's everyone else?'

'Our crowd? I don't know. Wherever the rest of the party is, I presume.'

'Good.' I gave them a brief outline of everything that had happened since we'd left the castle, with occasional interpolations from Jay and Alban to help things along. It was hardest to speak of Miranda.

Rob and Val listened in attentive silence, though their eyes widened at the part about the nine Britains. When we had finished, neither spoke for a few moments.

Then Val said a very rude word.

I looked at her in shock, for she was not usually one for profanity. But her eyes were shining, and she'd sat up straighter in her chair. 'The possibilities!' she breathed. Then her face darkened. 'How *could* they hide such a thing from us!'

I wondered who she meant by "us": people in general, or the Society? For that matter, who did she mean by "them"? Who in the sixth Britain knew anything about any of this? Probably the Ministry. The Troll Court, to a degree. Anybody else?

'That's for later,' said Rob rather curtly. 'First, we have to get out of here. How far is Millie's house?'

'Not far.' I eyed Val uneasily as I spoke, though, for she was not in her strongest state, and there was the cliff path to manage.

'Let's go, then,' said Rob, and took hold of Val's chair as though he meant to wheel it. The chair rose to its customary two inches off the floor, and hovered away towards the corridor, Rob there to guide it.

The *click-click* of claws on tiles split the silence, and my pup came bounding into the room, her tail high and furiously wagging. She frisked and gambolled about me like I was her favourite ever person and I could almost have cried.

I scooped her up and covered her soft little head in kisses.

When we exited the kitchen, there was no sign of Miranda, but I didn't mind. Some gratitude had blossomed, to balance out some of my negative feelings towards her. It couldn't mend the rift between us, but it was a start.

I had hoped to see Zareen and George once more before we left the castle, but there was no sign of them whatsoever. We were obliged to go on without a final farewell.

The journey back to the top of the cliff was, of necessity, rather slow, and I chafed at the delay. If the guests weren't escaping Millie's clutches by then, they were probably going quietly mad under the influence of her eccentric notions of entertainment. I might be eager to shuttle Ancestria Magicka out of here as soon as possible, but I did not want their collective insanity on my conscience.

To my relief, the first house we approached at the top of the cliff — one of the pale starstone ones, whose walls were beginning to glow with a serene, blue radiance as twilight approached — flung open its door, and beckoned us with another fanfare of light and music. From there, the distance to Millie's farmhouse was but a few steps, and we were back in the parlour.

Foolish woman! thundered a disembodied male voice as we tumbled into the room. *Stop this unseemly yowling at once. I must have silence.*

This is my ball! answered Millie with a shriek. *And I will not be interrupted!*

'I see Drystan's arrived,' I murmured, as we guided Val to a corner removed from much of the chaos of the parlour.

Jay sighed, and laid a soothing hand upon the wall. 'Millie,' he said with mild reproach, and began talking to her in an undertone.

I stopped listening, for I needed to think. I had swiftly given up on the idea of talking Melmidoc into excepting us from his general amnesiation plan, for I'd detected in him a stubbornness to rival my own, and we did not have days of spare time to spend arguing with him about it. But that presented an urgent problem.

I leaned nearer to the Baron. 'How are we to avoid Drystan's spell?'

'What, you don't have a plan? How is this possible.' He spoke teasingly but he was not looking at me: his gaze roamed the parlour, as though he was looking for something.

'Not yet. Every time I think about it I get distracted—what is it?' For a frown had descended and he looked, suddenly, troubled.

'Where's Fenella?' he said.

'Somewhere in the house?' I suggested. 'Not everyone is in the parlour. They must be spread all over the place.'

'We need to find her, immediately.'

'What's bothering you?'

'I've a hunch she might have given us the slip.'

The Baron, Rob and I spread out to search the house. It did not take long to establish that Alban was right: there was no sign of Fenella anywhere.

19

'Drystan!' I hissed, putting my lips close to the nearest wall. I was in the entrance hall of Millie's farmhouse. I did not know if proximity to the wall would help him to hear me any better, but it seemed worth a try. I had to repeat his name several times before I could get his attention, so intent was he upon his argument with Millie.

What is it? he snapped at last.

'We are missing one of our number, and the most dangerous one at that. We cannot begin until she's found.'

Describe her.

I did that, painting as vivid a picture of Fenella as I had last seen her as I could.

Drystan went quiet for a while, to Millie's delight, who began another song.

She is found, Drystan whispered to me. *Dulcina of Moondance Cottage has sighted her traversing the cliff's edge. It is thought that she is attempting to reach my brother's spire.*

Had she somehow guessed our intentions and fled from the farmhouse, or did she have some other purpose in mind for the spire? Either way, I wondered how she had managed to evade the allure of the many houses and cottages along the way. Not even I had accomplished that, despite being forewarned.

I bundled my precious pup into the Baron's arms and left the farmhouse at a run.

Melmidoc had parked his spire at the other end of the cliff road from Millie's farmhouse. It was not difficult to spot, for the sun was sinking fast and the Starstone Spire blazed with eerie, beautiful blue light. I suppose it proved a natural beacon for Fenella to aim for. Who wouldn't be intrigued by such a display?

I tore after her. My bare feet objected strenuously to this treatment, for the ground was stony and I had not time to take care where I placed my steps. But I gained steadily upon Fenella, ignoring the stinging of my lacerated feet and the heaviness in my limbs that tiredness had wrought.

It was only once I had almost caught her that I realised I, once again, had no plan. What was I going to do, haul her bodily back to the farmhouse? Hah. She was several inches taller than me, and I had no idea what her magickal capabilities were. For all I knew, she was a better practitioner than me, too.

'Fenella!' I shouted. 'This won't *do.*'

She glanced over her shoulder at me, but rather than stop and talk, as I had hoped, she only ran faster towards Melmidoc's spire. Once she knew herself pursued, she picked up speed and soon began to outpace me. Damn her and her long legs. It didn't help that I was winded and slowing down. I'm a walker more than a runner. It's not my talent.

Melmidoc, though, was awake. Fenella never reached the door, for when she got within ten feet of it, running at full tilt, she bounced off... something, and ended flat on her back on the ground, staring dazed at the darkening sky.

I am afraid I am invitation only, remarked Melmidoc.

Fenella snarled with chagrin, and stared up at me with blazing hatred. 'Bloody Society,' she spat. 'Must you destroy everything?'

'Actually,' I panted, my burning lungs drawing great gulps of air. 'I think it's you bidding fair to destroy everything.'

'I don't want to cause any harm.' She picked herself up slowly, touching a hand to her bloodied nose. 'I just want...'

'What?' I prompted. 'Everything you want will cause untold damage to this place, Fenella, and to our Britain as well. It doesn't matter whether that's the goal or not.'

She gave me a look of intense dislike and, without warning, began to run again.

I watched her go. I knew I didn't have it in me to catch her a second time.

My dismay was short-lived, however, for I found that I was not the only one who had come running after Fenella.

Millie had, too.

What can I say about what happened next? If you haven't seen an eighteenth-century farmhouse, front door agape, cackling in song as it chases down a fleeing woman, you truly haven't lived. I stood clutching my side, breathing painfully around the stitch in my insides and breathless with mirth as Millie-the-farmhouse bore down relentlessly upon poor Fenella Beaumont. She did not stand a chance. She *almost* made it to the top of the cliff path before the house snapped her up like a dog gobbling down a choice biscuit, and the door slammed shut upon her.

Trapping not quite everyone inside, for on the porch stood Rob and Jay and Baron Alban, maintaining a white-knuckled grip upon the pillars. Val's chair was slammed up against the low, white-painted railing that surrounded it. Fortunately, Val was still in it.

Whether they had come out with a view to joining the hunt for Fenella, or to avoiding Drystan's forgetting spell, was more or less moot, for it solved the latter problem either way. I limped up to the porch and sat down with my back against the door, wincing at the pain in my feet.

Drystan's voice came through the wall.

Interlopers all! he boomed. *I regret to inform you that you are not welcome here.*

'Let's just wait here for a bit, shall we?' I said, smiling up at my friends. From my recumbent posture upon the floor, they loomed over me even more than usual. Baron Alban stooped down and put the puppy back into my arms. She was sound asleep.

Jay was sceptical. 'You think he won't notice us out here?'

'He's got a lot of people in there to keep track of.' But for good measure I put up a shield around us, imbued with my best defences against magickal interference.

Jay's expression turned both withering and apprehensive, which cost me a pang.

But Alban relaxed against the wall, arms folded, a picture of serenity. 'Don't worry,' he said, grinning at me. 'Ves's shields are legendary.'

'We'll be fine,' I said confidently — wondering in private whether Alban was teasing me, or speaking the truth. Legendary? Really?

'Famous last words,' muttered Jay.

'OFFICIALLY,' I SAID A few hours later, 'None of us remembers anything.'

'I imagine that is wise, yes,' said Milady. 'Just how far from the truth is it?'

'That... varies.' We had escaped most of Drystan's spell, but not all of it. Bits of it had hit the five of us in different ways; I, for example, had forgotten half of Fenella's original speech until Alban had reminded me. Jay had had to be filled in again on the whole topic of Drystan's forgetting spells. We'd had to piece everything back together between us, which had taken some time. 'But I think we have more or less all of it straight again.'

We had already relayed much of it to Milady, but it had come out as a garbled mess, and it had taken contributions from all four of us (Rob, Val, Jay and me — Alban had already departed for Their Majesties' Court) to get through the tale. Whether we had been so incoherent due to the after-effects of Drystan's spell and the journey home, or merely due to exhaustion, I was too tired to say.

Millie Makepeace had whisked the lot of us back to our own, dear Britain, singing like a drunken lark all the way. She had dumped us not far from the erstwhile site of Ashdown Castle, and from there she could not be persuaded to move. So, we had been obliged to get ourselves back to our own House the long, tiring way. There had been more hitchhiking involved than I am ever happy about.

We'd left Ancestria Magicka and guests milling in confusion around the devastated lawns that had once hosted the proud pile of their castle. They would be fine. Their cars were still there, and most of them were even functional. What they would make of the absence of Ashdown, or how they would account for the gap of some hours between the high point of the party and their arrival back in the grounds, we did not wait to find out.

Milady had been shocked by our revelations. The Troll Court may have known about three of the Britains, but (if she was to be believed) Milady had known nothing about any of it. I knew she would need some time to think it over.

Our report concluded, I found I had sunk to the floor and sat with my back against the wall. An undignified posture, especially before Milady, but I was too wrecked to help it. 'Can we come Home?' I heard myself say.

I don't know what I had been planning to utter just then, but that wasn't it.

Milady was silent for longer than I liked. We, I should perhaps say, for I am pretty sure Jay was holding his breath, too.

'I'm sorry,' said Milady at length. 'I don't know that it is wise just at present. For one thing, two representatives from the Ministry were here yesterday, asking questions about the two of you. They want to talk to you. And for another, these Britains must be investigated. We cannot leave things as they are. I may need a few among you to go back to this fifth Britain, but this cannot now be done openly.'

I looked at Jay. I thought he might be pleased at this last reflection, having expressed a clear desire to stay behind with Melmidoc. But he sat looking at his hands, and said nothing.

I could understand the conflict. I, too, wanted very much to return to the fifth Britain. But I also wanted very much to return to the fold. I missed my Home.

'I will have decided by this afternoon,' said Milady. 'For now I urge you all to get some rest. You may use your old rooms for tonight, Ves, Jay, though I encourage you to avoid notice as much as possible. There's chocolate in all the pots.'

The word *all* had a promising ring to it, for we had left our pot behind at the Scarlet Courtyard. I put the problem of our immediate future out of my mind for the moment

— trying not to dwell upon how little I'd liked roguedom, when it came to it — and went to bed.

On the desk in my room, an enormous chocolate pot stood waiting, steam wisping from its spout. It was made from solid gold.

WHEN I SURFACED LATER that day, it was an insistent rapping on my door that roused me. I hauled myself out of bed with a groan, wrapped a blanket around myself, and answered the door with a bleary, 'Yes?'

Jay stood there, clad in jeans and a clean white shirt and looking far more bright-eyed than he had any right to be. Wordlessly, he handed me an envelope.

I carried it back to bed with me.

'Open it,' Jay urged, hovering awkwardly in the door-way.

'Oh, come in. I'm decent.'

He drifted exactly two steps farther into the room.

Thick, creamy paper made up the beautiful envelope, and another sheaf of the same fell out when I tore it open. The most perfect calligraphy I had ever seen covered the paper, complete with gilded flourishes.

I read quickly.

'Well?' said Jay, when I did not speak.

I dropped the pretty thing onto the bed, unable to muster a single word in reply. Maybe I was not yet awake.

I picked it up and read it all over again. Still the same. The pup, emerging sleepily from somewhere under the blankets, gave it a desultory sniff and sneezed.

'The Baron said he would call you when—' began Jay, just as my phone rang.

I answered it with a croak.

'Did you get the invitations?' said Baron Alban's deep voice.

Invitations? I glanced again at Jay, and saw that he had another such page in his hands. 'Are you sure *invitations* is the right word?' I said. 'I think such missives are typically termed *royal summons.*'

'Their Majesties can't issue you a royal summons, Ves. You and Jay are not among their subjects.'

'The nearest thing to it, then.'

'Mm. So, are you going to answer it?'

'Do we have a choice?'

'Technically.'

'What does that mean.'

'It means those two reps from the Ministry that were sniffing around after you have been invited to desist, and if you would like to avoid those kinds of complications recurring it might not hurt to have Their Majesties' Court at your backs for a while longer.'

I tried to decide whether there was an implied threat somewhere in there, and decided probably not. It wasn't Alban's style. He did, however, have a point.

'What are we supposed to do for Their Majesties, Alban?'

'You'll find out when you get here.'

'Nefarious or not?'

'Depends on who you ask.'

I met Jay's eye and mouthed the words, *yes or no*?

He held out his closed fist, thumb extended, and slowly turned it upwards.

'All right, we're in,' I said to the Baron.

'Fantastic. I'll pick you up at five.'

He rang off.

'So,' I said, staring with bemused eyes at the summons. 'What does one wear to be presented to royalty?'

'Shit,' said Jay, and glanced, dismayed, at his highly informal attire. 'No idea. What, the great Ves hasn't been presented to royalty before?'

'Not like this, and not these royals. It's the most powerful of the fae courts, and rarely open to outsiders.'

Jay looked impressed, and perhaps just a little terrified.

I probably looked much the same.

He swallowed. 'What do you suppose they want us to do for them?'

'I don't know,' I said, mustering my courage and my blanket both and heading for my wardrobe. 'But come hell or high water, I'm going to be well-dressed when we find out.'

Also By Charlotte E. English

Modern Magick

The Road to Farringale

Toil and Trouble

The Striding Spire

The Fifth Britain

Royalty and Ruin

Music and Misadventure

The Wonders of Vale

The Heart of Hyndorin

Alchemy and Argent

The Magick of Merlin

Dancing and Disaster

House of Werth

Wyrde and Wayward

Wyrde and Wicked

Wyrde and Wild